Zach almost laughed. And she still wouldn't look at him, and that's when he knew. He knew beyond a shadow of a doubt Mariah Stewart found him attractive.

Well, well, well.

Little miss animal rights activist was hot for him. He wasn't sure if he should be flattered...or scared.

"Don't worry," he said softly, closing the distance between them and tipping her

She gasped.

He tried not t e did it except mayb ng to do with the him insane with her comments and her innuendos and assumptions.

He pretended to examine her. "Your eyes aren't dilated or glazed over, so no hypoglycemia."

"That's good," she said softly.

"But if you fall down, I'll catch you."

He released her, and she blinked. He smiled. Oh, yeah. She found him attractive all right.

So what are you going to do about it?

Drive her crazy. Completely and utterly crazy. Maybe then she'd leave him alone.

Dear Reader,

Usually my book ideas are the result of a conversation I've overheard, or an idea suggested by a friend, but that wasn't the case with *A Cowboy Angel*. As a reporter for a local newspaper I was writing a story on the horse slaughter industry and its connection to horse racing. As I was working on the article I found myself thinking: *What if?*

What if a race horse owner met an activist? What if that activist hated horse racing? What if against all odds they started to fall in love?

I am a sucker for a horse tale. Throw in a hero with a passion for animals and I'm there. I had to pit that hero against a woman as outspoken as she was beautiful, but the resulting story, *A Cowboy's Angel,* the first book in a series set in the fictional town of Via Del Caballo, is everything I always strive for in a tale. Fun. Fast-paced and, most of all, a fabulous love story...or so I hope.

You might be interested to know that I own a horse that came from a horse slaughter auction. I recently won my first buckle with that horse—proof that even our four-legged friends can have a happily ever after.

Best,

Pam

P.S. Look for Jillian's story next!

A COWBOY'S ANGEL

PAMELA BRITTON

HARLEQUIN® AMERICAN ROMANCE®

ISBN-13: 978-0-373-75517-2

A COWBOY'S ANGEL

This edition published by arrangement with Harlequin Books S.A.

For questions and comments about the quality of this book, please contact us at CustomerService@Harlequin.com.

Printed in U.S.A.

ABOUT THE AUTHOR

With over a million books in print, Pamela Britton likes to call herself the best-known author nobody's ever heard of. Of course, that changed thanks to a certain licensing agreement with that little racing organization known as NASCAR.

But before the glitz and glamour of NASCAR, Pamela wrote books that were frequently voted the best of the best by the *Detroit Free Press,* Barnes & Noble (two years in a row) and *RT Book Reviews.* She's won numerous awards, including a National Readers' Choice Award and a nomination for the Romance Writers of America's Golden Heart® Award.

When not writing books, Pamela is a reporter for a local newspaper. She's also a columnist for the *American Quarter Horse Journal.*

Books by Pamela Britton

HARLEQUIN AMERICAN ROMANCE

985—COWBOY LESSONS
1040—COWBOY TROUBLE
1122—COWBOY M.D.
1143—COWBOY VET
1166—COWGIRL'S CEO
1285—THE WRANGLER
1322—MARK: SECRET COWBOY
1373—RANCHER AND PROTECTOR
1407—THE RANCHER'S BRIDE
1453—A COWBOY'S PRIDE
1476—A COWBOY'S CHRISTMAS WEDDING

HARLEQUIN HQN

DANGEROUS CURVES
IN THE GROOVE
ON THE EDGE
TO THE LIMIT
TOTAL CONTROL
ON THE MOVE

For Julie Craycroft

For sending Tiffany boxes, Halloween stickers, Christmas presents, and so many other things over the years. Thank you, Nanna. I can't tell you how much your little packages mean to my child. Without you she wouldn't know what it was like to have a grandmother. Thank you so much for stepping in and showing her the meaning of selfless love.

Chapter One

"So you're just going to kill the horse?"

Zach Johnson groaned.

"Couldn't you at least try to rehab him or something?"

Could this day get any worse?

He glanced at Doc Miller and his groom, Pat, their own faces frozen in what could only be called consternation. Nearby, horses stabled along the backstretch of Golden Downs raceway watched, too, with ears pricked forward as if curious what he would do.

Go ahead. Turn around, they seemed to say.

He didn't want to. He really didn't, but he knew if he ignored Mariah Stewart, she'd just come right around the front of him and start yammering in his face.

He slowly turned. "What makes you think I'm going to put him down?" he asked, wishing for the umpteenth time that she weren't so damn pretty. It irritated the hell out of him that someone so insufferable could be so attractive. Today her red hair glittered as brightly as her eyes beneath the blazing-hot Southern California sun. He found himself wondering where she'd gotten that cute little snub nose and tiny chin of hers…and the freckles. He'd always been a sucker for freckles.

"Don't you always?" She lifted an eyebrow and

crossed her arms over her chest. "Your type likes to toss away anything that doesn't make you money."

He resisted the urge to raise his eyes toward the clear blue sky. God wasn't going to help him on this one; he had better things to do.

"We've been over this before." He glanced at his vet, knowing the man had as little patience for the woman in jeans and her CEASE—Concerned Equestriennes Aiding in Saving Equines—T-shirt as Zach did himself. "I don't put my horses down."

She snorted.

"I send them to auction."

She uncrossed her arms. "Same thing."

Next to them, Black in a Dash, the pride of Triple J Quarter Horse Stables, groaned. They'd tranquilized him pretty good, the horse hanging his head, injured back leg just barely touching the ground. Torn suspensory. That was what Doc Miller had just diagnosed. An ultrasound had confirmed Zach's worst fears, yet even with the injury, Dasher would always have a home with him—not that she'd believe him if he told her that. Dasher was special. The last foal his dad had bred before his death. He wasn't sure how he'd afford feeding him if he wasn't out winning races, but he'd cross that bridge when he came to it.

"Please," he said to Mariah. "Can you leave us alone right now?" He glanced imploringly at Doc Miller.

The man seemed to take the hint. "As I was saying, euthanasia is *one* option." Doc Miller clearly directed his words toward Mariah and sounded as frustrated as Zach felt. "But since he's a well-bred stallion, you might want to keep him around."

He thought he heard Mariah snort again.

"Then again, with an injury like this he could make a comeback in a year or two. I know you were hoping to race him in the Million Dollar Futurity this fall, but I think that's out of the question, Zach. There's other races coming up, though. Heck, some are even for aged stallions, so it might not be a complete loss if he does make it back in a year or two. We could try some stem-cell therapy and shockwave treatments and see what happens, but it's a long shot, Zach—I'm not going to sugarcoat it. And it'll cost some money along the way."

Money he didn't have, Zach thought. He was land rich and cash poor.

For a moment he considered calling Terrence Whitmore and telling him he could have it all. The farm, his parent's home up on the hill, even all the broodmares—everything—just so he could be done.

"*I* want to buy him."

He just about groaned again. Zach almost, *almost,* turned and gave her a piece of his mind, but his mama's Southern upbringing stopped him cold—God rest her soul.

"He's not for sale."

"So what are you going to do? Use him to make more babies that will probably never be fast enough to race and that you'll send to some horrible auction where, as you say, someone will buy them, all the while knowing deep inside that the someone in question is *really* a representative of a foreign meat company that only wants your horse so he can serve it up on a dish in France."

Honestly, he was getting kind of tired of her spiel, but he held his tongue. She came around the front of him, blocking his view of Pat, who still held the lead line of his horse. "And if the horse isn't fast enough, you'll run it, likely ruining another good horse and tossing that one away, too." She flicked her hands at him in disgust. "It's a vicious cycle."

"Ma'am, like I said earlier, I'm not like that. Not at all. Now if you'll excuse me, I have a sick horse to tend to."

He touched his horse's black coat, stroking his smooth neck, admiring the way it glowed and then straightening a piece of black mane. For a stallion, Dasher was as well behaved as they came. He'd been looking forward to breeding him and passing along some of his easygoing personality, but if Dasher never had the opportunity to make a name for himself, nobody would care how good the stallion looked or how well he behaved. Without a winning pedigree, nobody would want to breed to him. Ever.

Damn it.

He fought against nausea and anxiety and an overwhelming sense of failure. Ever since his dad had died and he'd taken over the ranch, things had gone downhill.

"We'll get you healed up," he told the horse softly, but he didn't know if he was speaking to Dasher or reassuring himself. Hell, he might have even been telling that red-haired harridan. "Don't know if you'll ever race again, but Dad would roll over in his grave if I didn't at least give it a try."

"Glad to hear you say that." Doc Miller patted the horse's neck, too. "He's a good-looking stallion, Zach. I think he'll make a great sire. I'll send over my care instructions and some treatment options later. In the meantime, Pat, why don't you put him away? He looks about ready to fall over."

The groom did as instructed, Dasher as wobbly as a drunken race fan. Zach and Doc Miller watched him walk off, the both of them standing between two rows of stables, grooms walking horses back and forth, some in saddles, others wet from being hosed off after a hard workout. The smell of horse hung heavy in the air, a smell that usually soothed him. Not today.

With a sigh, he turned back to the veterinarian. "I appreciate your honesty."

The two men shook hands before the veterinarian headed out. Zach thought he was alone until he heard that Stewart woman say from behind him, "So you're *not* going to put him down?"

Though he told himself not to, he still sighed.

"I told you, no." He heard his heel grind into the dirt as he turned. "It should be pretty obvious I'm not like other owners." He motioned to the barn aisle behind them. "I only have three of my own horses in training and two for other people. Do I look like a big-time operation?"

She followed his gaze. He took in the red-and-gold stall boards nailed to the top doors—a JJJ in the middle of a triangle, their brand—and red hay nets filled with premium alfalfa hanging next to them. Pat was just putting Dasher in his stall. They both watched as he unhooked the nylon webbing that kept the horses inside without them having to close the heavy wooden bottom door. Though he might have been drugged, Dasher immediately turned toward his hay net, ears lazily pricked forward. It never failed. A horse had to be pretty sick not to eat. Dasher wasn't sick, just really, really lame.

The nausea returned.

"Well," he heard Mariah say, "you might not have as many horses as the other owners, but that doesn't mean you don't adhere to the same mind-set."

She turned back to face him and once again he couldn't help but notice she was cute, maybe even beautiful—if one liked loudmouthed shrews, which he didn't.

"I don't have as many horses because I don't breed as many. My dad adhered to the concept of quality, not quantity. It's a principle I still believe in."

And that wasn't making him any money, but he'd come up with something. Maybe Mr. Whitmore would be interested in a few of his broodmares. He had a couple yet that didn't have foals by their sides....

"Quality, not quantity, yet you still sell your unwanted horses at auction."

He let loose a sigh of impatience. Why did he bother? What did it matter what she thought of him?

Yet for some reason...it did.

"A reputable auction," he explained. "A place where our horses have a chance of finding a new owner, and not the kind of owner that will turn around and sell our horses to the slaughter market you mentioned earlier. We give our unwanted horses a second chance at life, Ms. Stewart."

Her brows lifted. "You know my name."

"Doesn't everyone?"

"I hope so." She raised her chin. "I hope people think of me as the voice of their unwanted horses. I hope racehorse owners have me on their mind when they sell their animals directly to a meat-processing company. I hope racehorse owners think of me when they travel to a foreign country and see *cheval* on the menu. Most of all, I hope you know I'm watching you and your ilk."

Her passion was unmistakable, as was the determination in her golden-brown eyes. There was something else there, too, a lingering sense of sadness that seemed to call to him in some bizarre and unexpected fashion.

"Do you always make generalizations about people?"

"Excuse me?"

"I could do the same thing and call you a crazy crackpot activist, but I don't."

She propped her hands on her hips. "We only act crazy out of frustration. No matter how loud we scream, the racehorse industry just keeps breeding more and more horses."

"Something they've been doing for centuries."

"Doesn't make it right."

"And I suppose it's right to block the entrance of the track so people can't get to work?"

"We were trying to make a statement." She flicked her long hair back.

"And picketing on race day?"

"It got everyone's attention."

He bit back a sigh of frustration. He could have sworn he heard her do the same thing, too.

"Clearly, your tactics aren't working."

"I know."

"So why do it?"

"Because I've seen ten ex-racehorses crammed into the back of a four-horse trailer, panic in their eyes, open sores on their bodies from being kicked and bullied and knocked over by the other horses, barely able to stand because they haven't been given any water, their once proud carriage completely demoralized. And it's sad and it's sick and I don't want it happening anymore."

His stomach turned. Yeah, he'd heard of that kind of stuff happening, too, but not to his horses, no way.

But could he say with absolute certainty that one of his horses *hadn't* ended up that way?

No.

"Look," she said, and when their gazes met, hers had softened, almost as if she'd spotted his guilty conscience. "If you really are different like you say you are, I have a proposition for you."

She wanted to proposition him? Suddenly, crazily, his mood improved, although what he was thinking probably wasn't the kind of proposition she had in mind.

"What kind of proposition?"

"Actually, it's more like I want to discuss something with you, an idea I've been floating around. Not here." She glanced past him. He could see a groom approaching with another wet horse, its coat glistening as if it were made of glass. "Later. At your farm."

It was his turn to be surprised. She knew where he lived? Well, maybe that wasn't so strange after all. She probably had a map on her bedroom wall, red dots marking where all the evil racehorse breeders lived, their pictures next to them, horns probably drawn onto their heads.

For that reason alone he should brush her off, but then he thought maybe for that reason alone he should do something unexpected. Hell, what did he have to lose? Maybe she'd "proposition" him with buying a few of his retired racehorses. Wouldn't that be something?

As if reading his mind, she said, "It's a way for maybe both of us to make some money."

He should say no. Despite how much he could use the cash, he should tell her he wasn't interested.

But with Dasher out of commission…

"Fine. Dinner. Tonight at six." He turned away before he could change his mind.

"Wait. *What?* Dinner?"

He almost laughed. Eating with the enemy?

"What's the matter?" He turned and cocked a brow. "Afraid I'll poison your food?"

She drew back. "No. Of course not. I just—"

Didn't want to think of him as a person. He saw that much in her eyes. Much better to keep him at arm's length. He didn't know for certain that was what she was thinking, but he had a pretty good idea because frankly, he'd had the same thought.

"Scared?"

"No."

"Then what's the problem?"

"Okay, fine." She sucked in a bottom lip, Zach watching as she nibbled it and then let it back out again. When she released the flesh, it was glossy and he found himself wondering how she'd taste.

Now you really have *lost your mind.*

"Can I bring anything?" she asked.

A negligee with frilly underwear.

Good Lord. Stop it.

"Just yourself."

It was that damn red hair of hers. And the freckles. He turned away before she caught a glimpse of what he was thinking in his eyes.

"Thank you, Mr. Johnson. I promise, you won't regret this."

Actually, he already did.

Chapter Two

Mariah was as anxious as a cat in a room full of dogs as she drove down a lonely country road three hours later. Low-lying hills long since turned brown by the hot summer sun surrounded her. It was a view she usually enjoyed. Not today.

He'd agreed to see her.

Okay, okay, so there was the little matter of dinner. Any other owner and it'd be no big deal. Any other owner was at least sixty years old and could have easily been her dad. Zach Johnson couldn't be much older than her twenty-six years and was, gosh darn it all, *good-looking.*

Thank God he had no clue how much he affected her.

She bashed her hand against the steering wheel of her ancient Honda Civic. She hated the fact that every time she spotted him at the racetrack, she found herself first noticing his tight jeans—and the nicely sculpted rear beneath—before she took note of the horses he schooled from the rail. The man was a bona fide hottie. She'd had that very conversation with her fellow CEASE members more than once, their discussion always ending with too bad he was a racehorse owner. It drove them crazy that anyone with the dark good looks of a soap opera star could race horses for a living. Not just race them but breed them and raise them, too. In some ways he was worse because he was one of the people responsible for the skyrocketing number of unwanted horses, those horses that would never be raced and that would ultimately end their days in the back of a makeshift horse trailer, transported to Mexico, where they would suffer at the hands of a meat processor.

Her stomach twisted.

Not if she could help it.

Up ahead the sign for the Triple J Ranch came into view. It was nestled in the heart of Via Del Caballo, California, and the land alone was worth millions. The residents of the area called it horsey central—with good reason. Farms were everywhere, their white fences intersecting the landscape as if God played an aerial game of tic-tac-toe. And what wasn't horse farms was vineyards. The Triple J was right in the middle of it all. She'd looked them up on the internet once upon a time, back when she'd first spotted Zach Johnson at Golden Downs and been told who he was. Second-generation racehorse breeder. Quarter horses, not Thoroughbreds, which meant he specialized in sprinters. The fastest animal in a quarter mile, their breeders often touted. That wasn't exactly true, but it made for great PR.

Her tires lost purchase on the gravel near the entrance to the ranch as she slammed on the brakes, nearly missing the turn. She cursed inwardly. Not paying attention. Too distracted by thoughts of Mr. Magnificent.

White fence rails guided her down a long straight road, one with trees on either side. To her left and right were pastures with emerald-colored grass clipped down by grazing horses. The two pastures were at least twenty acres apiece. Up ahead, perched atop a small knoll, was the main house, a huge behemoth of a structure whose windows caught the sun's last rays turning them gold. Originally it'd been a single A-frame, but his parents had completely renovated the place by the early '90s. Some said the remodel had caused Zach's parents' divorce.

That last part was track gossip, but she believed it because she'd heard from a number of sources that Samantha Johnson had damn near bankrupted the ranch after having the place overhauled, and then she'd run off with the general contractor, leaving James Johnson to raise his son. When he'd died two years ago, Zach had inherited the two-hundred-acre ranch, the racing operation and a pile of debt. More track gossip, only this time she wasn't certain if it was true.

The place was stunning. Certainly well kempt. At the end of a drive sat a horseshoe turnaround. A sign pointed her to the right, the word Office painted in gold against a red backdrop. She followed the directions. A parking area had been set up straight ahead. A single-story barn stood to the left, and to her right, a flat-roofed building, the office, she presumed. She pulled up next to a golf cart already parked in a spot between the two structures. Another white fence stretched between the two buildings, yet another pasture on the other side. On the top rail someone had posted a reserved sign where the golf cart had been parked.

"Here we go," she muttered, then took a deep breath, wondering if she should have driven up to the house and parked there. Great. He was probably watching her from his dining room window wondering what the hell she'd been thinking to park down at his barn. She almost backed out of the spot, but movement caught her eye.

Zach Johnson.

Her breath caught. He stood at the entrance to the barn, a straw cowboy hat on his head, his eyes shielded by the brim, but not his lower jaw. Its strong outline could be seen clearly, as could his mouth, razor stubble growing above and around it. He was one of those men who always seemed to have a five-o'clock shadow, no matter if it was seven in the morning or eight at night. Dark hair. Dark eyes. She'd always thought them brown until she'd noticed today they were a dark, dark blue, made darker by the thick black lashes that surrounded them.

Lord help her.

"Glad you didn't go up to the house," he said as she slowly stepped out of her car, the black short-sleeved shirt he wore revealing tan arms. "I'm in the middle of feeding. You want to tag along?"

Good-looking, friendly and willing to talk to her about how they might save unwanted racehorses' lives.

"Oh, um…" *Not really.* "Sure," she called back, hoping he didn't see the way she wilted against the side of her car.

Maybe having dinner with him was a bad idea.

Go on. Move. He's not going to bite.

No, but she wished he would bite the side of her neck, maybe suckle it—

Stop it, stop it, stop it, stop it.

Why, oh why, did the man have this kind of effect on her? It was crazy how every time she saw him, her heart would beat like the skin of a drum. Her palms would grow sweaty. And her body would buzz and warm in places it had no business buzzing and warming. None at all.

"Come on. We'll use the golf cart. I already fed the barn."

He walked toward her. All she could do was nod and then push away from the side of her car.

Get a grip.

Sexual attraction. Inconvenient, inconceivable, stupid sexual attraction. In college she'd had the hots for one of her professors. Eventually it'd worn off. Hopefully, this would, too.

"Um, nice place." She ducked beneath the canvas roof of the cart as she climbed in next to him and he smelled… Oh, he smelled *sooooo* nice. Like sage and sawdust with a hint of sweat.

"Thanks." He started the engine, the reverse gear popping into place with a jerk, something that seemed to be universal to golf carts the world over. "My parents built the barns and the fencing, but the house is original to the property."

Should she admit she knew that? Wouldn't he find that stalkerlike? "I read about that on your website."

He glanced at her quickly. Yup. Definitely thought her stalkerlike.

"I research all the racehorse owners."

Beneath his straw hat, a mixture of amusement and devilry shone in his skyline-colored eyes. "Oh, I'm sure. I bet you have dossiers on all of us."

He shifted the cart into first gear, and she had a feeling he looked away only because he'd been about to laugh.

"It's nothing personal."

Why are you defending yourself? Geez, get a grip.

Because it was personal with him, she admitted, and all because of this damn ridiculous physical attraction. She'd known it from the start too. Usually, she went online to find out more about a racing stable's operations—the number of stallions they had, if they bred their own broodmares, how many foals dropped in a year, that kind of thing. She'd be lying, though, if she didn't admit to clicking around on the Triple J Ranch's website looking for more information about Zach. What had he called himself? Small-time? Something like that, and they were. The Triple J Ranch could easily house dozens of racehorses, but she'd only counted four broodies out front. They didn't have a stallion at stud, either. She'd heard they'd had to put him down a couple years ago, but she couldn't deny that all that information had been secondary to finding out if he had a wife or kids or a girlfriend.

She was such an idiot.

"Sorry about your horse," she blurted, because there she went blushing again. They were driving toward a shed, one that served as cover for the pasture animals on one side and looked to be some kind of storage facility on the other side. "Bad luck."

"You have no idea."

A soft breeze wafted across her face. It blew the smell of him away from her and allowed her to focus more on what she was at the Triple J to do.

Thank God.

"If Doc Miller suggests a fasciotomy, don't do it."

She felt him glance over at her. She was trying to keep her eyes straight ahead, but it was hard to resist the urge to turn and meet his gaze.

"It's an unproven procedure that might end up doing more harm than good."

Don't look at him. Do not *look at him.*

She looked at him.

Zap!

That was what his stare felt like. Zing. Zoom. Zam.

"More internet research?" he teased.

Breathe.

"Actually," she all but wheezed, "I'm a vet."

He slammed on the brakes. She had to throw her hands forward to avoid slipping off the seat.

"What?"

They'd made it to the shed, but one glimpse into his eyes and she realized she'd shocked him. Good. If she kept him on his toes, maybe then he wouldn't spot the way she blushed every time their gazes met.

"A vet. Graduated two years ago. That's part of what I wanted to talk to you about. I have some ideas about the aftercare of horses with an injury like Dasher's."

She really wished he would quit looking at her like that. It made her all kinds of uncomfortable and...quaky inside. Yes, quaky, especially since she was closer than she'd ever been to him before. She could see up close how perfectly his features all melded together into a picture of utter male handsomeness.

"Where's your practice?"

"I don't... Well, I mean, I do have one. I mean, I could if I wanted to, and I do, sort of...."

She took a deep breath. "I work for nonprofits, mostly. Did a year in Mexico and Chile gelding stallions for rural farmers. These days I'm focusing on problems that are closer to home. I work for a temp agency that specializes in placing veterinarians. It means I have to travel a lot, but that's okay. Working temp jobs gives me lots of free time to focus on CEASE."

There. That hadn't sounded so bad. He didn't need to know that she'd been looking for full-time work for months now. Let him think she selflessly devoted herself to her cause.

He turned off the cart. “Be right back.”

“What? Wait. I’ll go with you.”

“No, no. Just stay there.”

He left her there sitting all alone.

She slumped against the seat in disappointment. She’d been hoping for a “Good for you,” maybe even a “Wow, I’m impressed,” but all she saw was his impressive backside disappear inside the shed.

You should be grateful he put some distance between the two of you.

Instead she dwelled on her disappointment at his nonreaction, and that worried her all the more. What did she care if he wasn’t impressed by her vocation? He was a racehorse owner. The enemy.

A handsome enemy.

She covered her face with her hands and groaned. She had the hots for him, all right. And she had them bad.

“Not good,” she heard herself say.

Not good at all.

A VET.

Zach pulled the string on a brand-new bag of grain, the threads sliding free with a *pop-pop-pop-pop,* all the while trying to figure out what would make a woman go through years and years of schooling only to toss them all away and found an organization like CEASE.

Crazy.

Well, he knew that. Everyone at Golden Downs knew it. When she and her buddies had picketed the entrance to the track, she’d arrived in a horse costume, complete with long flowing mane made out of yarn.

Crazy.

Outside he heard the rhythmic thud of horses’ hooves.

Belle and Baby must have spotted his arrival and were now galloping to the shelter in anticipation of gorging themselves on grain. One of them nickered along the way.

"Hold on, hold on," he said, opening a feed door along the back wall. Two anxious faces stared back at him, ears pricked forward, eyes bright. He smiled. "Did you honestly think I would forget about you?"

They nodded their heads as if answering his question but were really just exhibiting equine impatience, manes flying, forelocks waving. He poured out the feed. They acted starved. The two of them had all the grass in the world, but he gave them supplements to help the growth of their unborn foals.

"Slow down, you guys. You're going to choke."

"I, ah, I think I'm going to head on up to the house."

He just about jumped. His horses, too, both of them lifting their heads as if to ask, "Who's that?"

A pain in his backside.

She stood in the doorway, her pretty hair lit up like a sorrel-colored horse. He'd never seen hair such a golden-red before and not for the first time he wondered if it was fake or natural. He would bet natural.

"I brought something I should warm up, and so if you don't mind..." She motioned back toward the parking area. "I don't want it sitting in the sun, either."

"Hang on. I'll drive you."

He tossed the horses some grain, then all but threw the scooper back into the garbage can he used to store their feed and closed the lid with a snap before turning back around and brushing by her, their arms grazing. She jumped as if he'd hit her with flames.

It drew him up short. “Did I scratch you or something?”

“No, no.” She wouldn’t meet his gaze. “I’m fine. Just a little off-balance.”

He spotted the blush then. Saw how her pulse beat at the base of her neck. The way her gaze darted all over the place—anywhere but at him.

She was aware of him.

He stepped closer. “You sure you’re okay?”

She nodded. “Oh, yeah. Great. Just hungry. That’s why I want to start heating up my dish. I didn’t have any lunch and I’m starved. I’m such an idiot sometimes. I really should eat. Surprised I don’t just keel over sometimes.” She made the sound of a splat, using her forearm to mimic falling over. “Plop. That’s going to be me one day. Not eating makes me light-headed. That’s all.”

Who was she trying to convince? Him? Or her?

He almost laughed. And she still wouldn’t look at him, and that was when he knew. He knew beyond a shadow of a doubt she found him attractive.

Well, well, well.

Little Miss Animal-Rights Activist was into him. He wasn’t sure if he should be flattered…or scared.

“Don’t worry,” he said softly, closing the distance between them and tipping her chin up.

She gasped.

He tried not to laugh. He had no idea why he did it except maybe he supposed it had something to do with the number of times she’d driven him insane with her actions and her comments and her innuendos and assumptions.

He pretended to examine her. “Your eyes aren’t dilated or glazed over, so no hypoglycemia.”

“That’s good,” she said softly.

"But if you fall down, I'll catch you."

He released her. She blinked. He smiled. She turned the same color as her hair.

Oh, yeah. She found him attractive, all right.

So what are you going to do about it?

Drive her crazy, he told himself. Completely and utterly crazy. Maybe then she'd leave him alone.

Chapter Three

She couldn't get out of there fast enough.

Mariah ran back to her car while he finished up with the pasture horses. With any luck, she'd have gained control of her emotions by the time they met up again, at least she hoped so, anyway, as she pulled to a stop in front of his home. She found herself pausing for a moment after reaching between the passenger seat and driver's seat and grabbing a brown bag with her hors d'oeuvres.

She peered out the front windshield in curiosity. His home was gorgeous. A real showplace. Absolutely nothing of the original ranch remained. The outside consisted of three A-frames that sat side by side, with the middle portion bigger than the rest. Redwood siding complemented the massive windows along the front. The landscaping alone had to have cost 100 grand.

When she opened the car door and stepped outside, she could smell the redwood mulch used to line the planters of the gardens.

At least she didn't smell him anymore.

He'd told her to go on inside, but it still felt odd to open one of the double doors.

"Wow."

Okay. There was nice, and then there was *niiiice. Cavernous* didn't begin to describe the place. Huge beams supported the middle-section roofline—like the rib cage of a dinosaur. A parquet floor stretched from the fireplace on her right to the entertainment center on her left. Straight ahead a trio of windows overlooked the backside of the ranch with a stunning view of low-lying mountains outside.

"Must be nice," she heard herself mutter, heading to the left, where she could see the gleam of state-of-the-art kitchen appliances. After vet school she'd inherited a pile of debt and a liability insurance policy the size of a mortgage. It was why she didn't have her own practice. Not yet, anyway. By the time she made her student loan payment and paid the rent and insurance, not to mention a medical truck payment, she'd be lucky to clear five hundred dollars a month, not enough to live off, and certainly not enough to start her own business. Getting hired by an established vet—someone who could split expenses with her—was the first step toward that happening. And so she waited, and in the meantime she filled in for vacationing veterinarians whenever she could, which wasn't nearly as often as she needed. Thus the old jalopy outside.

The kitchen was just as spacious and grandiose as the foyer. Stainless-steel everything, light brown countertops with spots like quail eggs, tile on the floor instead of parquet. She set the bag down on the island in the middle, almost afraid to make a mess. If this was being small-time, where did she sign up?

Five minutes later she had just finished stirring the Parmesan cheese into her spinach dip when she heard the front door open.

Oh, dear.

Two seconds later he walked into the kitchen, the smell of him reaching her before he did: it wasn't shavings she'd smelled on him earlier, but some kind of fresh-cut grass and sweat and some sort of pine-scented aftershave that had caused her just as much discomfort inside as it had outside.

"Whatever that is, it looks delicious." He cocked his cowboy hat back a bit and peered into the dish. "What is it?"

He was tall. She liked tall men. They made her feel feminine and secure and somehow safe.

He's a racehorse owner, the sane part of her screamed. Heck, and a horse trainer, too.

But he'd agreed to let her help him. That meant something.

"It's cheesy spinach dip." She tried like heck not to edge away from him, but she could feel the heat radiate off of him, which, in turn, made *her* feel flush. "There's enough calories in that to clog an artery or two."

He leaned down close to her, so close she could see the dark blue ring around his eyes. "You trying to kill me, then?"

He could have no way of knowing how just being next to him was killing her. No way at all, but she could have sworn she saw the glimmer of something in his eyes, something that made her skin prickle.

"It's really good." She sounded like a timid little girl.

He had really white teeth and a smile that made it difficult to hold his gaze. "What do we dip?"

She pointed with her chin toward the brown bag. The moment he stepped away, the muscles in her shoulders collapsed. Her legs damn near did, too.

He found the pieces of the French loaf she'd cut up earlier, his look of pleasure as he dipped a fluffy piece of bread, lifted it to his mouth, then chewed doing strange things to her insides.

"Forget dinner. We should eat this."

"That's okay with me."

He smiled. "Nah. I have something special planned. Braised short ribs with a port arsenic reduction."

It took her a moment to follow his words, which just went to show how discombobulated she was. "Uh-huh."

All right. So he made her feel all silly and tongue-tied and teenager-like inside. Oh, well. She'd get over it.

"Just kidding."

He was? She straightened in embarrassment. How had she missed that?

You were too busy ogling him.

"Seriously," he said. "I'm making fajitas. Simple." He went to the fridge and began pulling out the ingredients—a package of beef, a bell pepper, an onion and grated cheddar cheese—and then set them on the island next to her brown bag. "Only takes a moment. Sit down while I brown the meat and onions. You can tell me your plans for Dasher."

She told herself to focus on what she'd come to do, not how the light from a window along the front of the house cast a glow onto his face, highlighting the dusky outline of his whiskers. He had a chin right out of a comic book and the shoulders to match. Hours out of doors had turned his skin a deep mahogany that emphasized the cobalt of his eyes. He kept peeking at her as he unwrapped the meat and set it on a cutting board.

"Go on," he encouraged.

She took a deep breath. *Okay. Focus.*

"I bet Dr. Miller suggested stall rest and some kind of therapy for Dasher."

He nodded as he began chopping the meat. "And maybe surgery."

"Don't listen to him."

He paused. "You care to tell me why I shouldn't listen to a doctor with thirty years of experience caring for racehorses?"

"For exactly that reason." She spotted a barstool beneath the center island far enough away from where he stood that maybe she could concentrate. "He's old-school."

"What's wrong with that?"

How could someone so handsome do something so deplorable for a living? It was hard to reconcile the man in front of her—good-looking, cooking dinner for her—and the mental image she'd built up of him as some kind of evil ogre.

"I wrote a paper my senior year on high suspensory tears in equines. In it I completely disproved the validity of the traditional treatment options used by modern-day veterinarians." She frowned. "Although not without ruffling a few feathers."

Including Paul's, but she wasn't going to think about that.

"I'll bet," he said, pulling a pan from somewhere and scraping the meat into it. "You're good at ruffling feathers." But he shot her a smile meant to take the sting out of his words, his grin causing her to shift her gaze to the granite counter. No, not granite, marble, she suddenly realized.

"They didn't like that I was right." When she lifted her gaze, it was in time to see him turn away, pan in hand, the *click-click-click* of the gas burner filling the air. "I might not have had as large a control group as they wanted, but I proved that conventional medical treatment guaranteed no more success than my method. In fact, my method actually had more success, something the review board chalked up to luck."

And it still burned her when she thought about it. Luck. As if fate had had something to do with the successful rehabilitation of two show horses.

"And what is that method?"

The sizzle of cooking meat made her stomach growl. She reached for a piece of bread and scooped a bit of the dip. She was pleased with how good it tasted.

"Let me ask you something." She resisted the urge to snatch up another piece. "If you were to tear your ACL or your meniscus, what do you think the doctors would prescribe as treatment?"

His back was still toward her as he shrugged, and Mariah couldn't help noticing the muscles beneath his polo shirt. They were as well defined as a professional boxer's. Must be all that hay he lifted.

"Rest. If that didn't work, surgery." She watched as he moved the meat around the pan. "Therapy afterward."

"Exactly." She gave in and scooped up more of the dip. Chewing gave her a moment to gather her thoughts. "Therapy. But what do they suggest you do? Lock your horse up for months on end, then walk him for another two months. No turnout. No movement. No real exercise. Nothing but rest, and that's not good for an animal that's genetically programmed to roam the range. Keep them cooped up for a few weeks and what happens?"

He turned, glancing up at her as he grabbed the onion pieces. "They blow."

"Exactly," she pronounced again. "And then you're right back where you started from, sometimes in an even worse position. I've seen some injured horses go crazy in their stalls from lack of activity. So you drug them, but you can only keep them drugged for so long before they have health problems, and then what?"

He went back to cooking and it smelled divine, especially when he grabbed some spices from a rack above the stove. The scent of whatever he sprinkled caused her to close her eyes and inhale.

"So what do you suggest we do for Dasher?"

She had to force herself to open her eyes, because it was far easier to concentrate when she wasn't looking at him. "Minimal stall rest, enough time to let the injury heal, then right back to work. Not," she quickly interjected, "regular work, but therapeutic activity, the same type of therapy your own doctor might prescribe. Stretches, leg lifts, weights, followed by massages and hot-and-cold therapy."

"You going to put Dasher on a treadmill, too?"

"I just might."

Once again he turned around and she couldn't mistake the laughter in his eyes, or the curiosity. He might be somewhat distracted cooking his scrumptious-smelling fajitas, but not so much that he hadn't heard what she had to say. What felt like butterfly wings brushed against her stomach. She had to look away, for fear he'd see the pleasure in her eyes.

He's the enemy. Best to remember that.

"My research shows it's important to keep a horse moving."

Too bad her professors had dismissed her findings. As if torn suspensories grew on trees. It would take years to compile enough data to appease them. Meanwhile, horses would continue to languish.

She shook her head. "Just like for a human, a lack of movement can cause the supporting tendons and muscles to atrophy. Standing still is the last thing you want them to do."

He went to the refrigerator and pulled out tortillas, then went back to stirring the pan.

"So what you're saying is you'd like me to do the *exact opposite* of what Doc Miller says." He picked up the pan and flipped all the ingredients like a master chef, and Mariah tried hard not to seem impressed when he glanced back at her afterward. "I'm supposed to just trust you."

Well, when he put it that way…

"I know it's a lot to ask, but I also know I'm right."

With a quick flick of his wrist, he turned off the stove, pulled out a pot holder from a drawer, tossed it on the counter, then set the steaming pan down on top of it.

"That smells so good," she said.

"Help yourself." He motioned toward the tortillas.

"No, no. You go first."

"Absolutely not. Ladies first."

A gentleman. Figured he'd be the exact opposite of what she'd expected.

"There's cilantro in the bag there if you want some." He pointed. "Oh, and I have salsa, too." He moved to the fridge and pulled a jar off a shelf. "Here."

She piled some meat and veggies onto a tortilla, hardly paying attention to what she grabbed because he was right next to her again and she'd begun to realize that being close to him was dangerous to her peace of mind.

"Thanks," she said.

Why did he have to be a racehorse owner? Why couldn't he have been a regular horse trainer? The kind that showed animals. One of the good ones, because even show-horse trainers could be bad. He wasn't. He was a racehorse trainer and owner. So she found herself ducking her head and trying like the devil not to notice how gorgeous his eyes were and how his smile came with dimples.

She couldn't retreat to the far end of the island fast enough. She nearly lost her appetite when he took a seat next to her.

"Do you like it?"

Had she taken a bite? Goodness, she hadn't even noticed. "Yes. It's great."

And it was. Great cook. Good man. Gorgeous dimples. *Crap.*

She'd finished half her plate before she said another word, and then only to say, "Thanks for cooking."

"My pleasure."

Was there any way she could get up and move without seeming rude? Probably not. So she forced herself to stop eating and say, "I really think with a few months of therapy, Dasher could be sound enough to ride. Not to race, of course, but good enough to go on to a career as a show horse or something. I'd want to see the ultrasounds Dr. Miller took today, of course, just to make sure, but I don't anticipate I'll change my mind. A torn suspensory is a torn suspensory."

"I'll have them for you first thing in the morning."

"It's okay. Take your time. He's going to need at least a month off. Then we'll get to work."

"You're going to help me rehab him?"

"Of course. Why wouldn't I?"

She couldn't take it anymore. She hopped up, scooping her plate up with her. "I'll do your dishes for you."

"Hell, no, you won't." He jumped up, too, grabbing her arm and turning her around midstep. "Let me take that."

Instinctively, she pulled her arm back. He closed the distance and reached for her plate. Their midsections brushed. Her cheeks heated like a nuclear reactor. She tried to step away, but the counter kept her from moving.

"Thanks," he said softly, taking the plate from her and setting it on the counter behind her.

Should she dart past him? Push him out of the way? What?

The man clearly read the dilemma in her eyes.

"Now what are you going to do?" he teased softly.

Chapter Four

If she'd still been holding the plate, she would have smashed it over his head, Zach thought, trying not to laugh.

"Let me go."

Her whole body had tensed. Her eyes briefly darted to his lips. She couldn't look at them for long.

Maybe it was all the times she'd caused him grief at the track. Maybe it was because she tried so hard to pretend there was nothing between them when it was clear as day that there was. Whatever the reason, he liked messing with her. Something about her gorgeous red hair and flashing brown eyes. Something that challenged him. No. Something that *defied* him. Her eyes seemed to silently accuse him of pushing her buttons on purpose…and he did.

"I thought you had a *proposition* for me," he whispered.

He saw her gulp, as if she suspected he meant a different type of proposition but didn't dare call him on it. "I do."

Her hands had stopped pushing. They lay flat against him in a spot somewhere between his breastbone and his abdomen, and it was all he could do not to bring their lower sections together again. Then he felt it, the gentle flexing of her fingers, the tips of them pressing against his chest, sliding downward.

Agh.

He let go. But when he looked in her eyes, he knew. She'd known exactly the type of proposition he'd had in mind—and it'd infuriated her.

"My *proposition* was to treat *all* of your injured horses, not just Dasher." She was shorter than him but somehow she managed to look down her nose. "I recognize they're under the care of Dr. Miller, but I can help them in a way he can't, free of charge."

He'd gone from being amused to feeling like a putz in two seconds flat. "How do you know I have more than one injured horse?"

"Track gossip says you have three, and that one of them is still undiagnosed despite spending a small fortune in vet fees."

Holy—he'd have to talk to his staff about blabbing to perfect strangers.

"One of them had a fractured sesamoid. There's not much you can do about that."

"Maybe. Maybe not. Why don't you let me decide that?"

"When?"

"The sooner we start, the better."

He should tell her no. He didn't need her poking around in even more of his business. Lord, for all he knew, this might be a ploy. A way for her to get into his business. To find something she and her friends at CEASE could use against him and maybe other horse breeders.

"Look, I appreciate the offer, but I can't exactly afford to pay you for experimental vet care. With Dasher out of commission it's going to make it hard for ends to meet as it is."

"I told you, there's no need to pay me." She crossed her arms in front of her. "I'll do it all for free."

Wow. She must really want to get the dirt on him.

Yet as he stared into her eyes, he didn't think that was true. She didn't look at him with malice in her eyes. Sure, she might still be irked over his whole "proposition" comment, but that wasn't what this was about. She stared up at him earnestly, and he could tell she waited with bated breath for him to answer.

Free vet care.

He'd spent a small fortune on Summer, the bay filly he'd been hoping to race and then breed. They'd found nothing wrong. Doc Miller had suggested he haul the horse up to UC Davis for a full-body scan, something he had neither the time nor the money to do, and it'd been heart-wrenching to admit they couldn't do anything else for her. He'd still breed her when she was old enough, but if he could discover what was wrong…

"Be here tomorrow around ten. I'll pop in after morning workouts and show you what we've got."

She hadn't expected him to agree. He saw her golden-brown eyes widen for a moment.

But then she relaxed. "Okay, then," she said with a glance toward the food she'd brought. "I'll just pick that up tomorrow."

"You're leaving?"

"Dinner was great."

She sidled toward the door.

He leaned back against the counter and asked a question that had been on his mind all afternoon. "Why?"

She paused. "Why, what?"

"Why are you doing this?"

She stood in his kitchen, her red hair so wild and untamed his fingers itched to grab a curl and tug it. The tips of it sparkled like the depths of a fire opal, the gold flecks matching the sparkle in her eyes.

"I want what's best for your horses. All horses. So many ex-racehorses are tossed away, but if we could get yours better, send them on to second careers, it might help your bottom line and help me to prove there's no need to kill a horse simply because it can't race again. Plus, if something I do helps them, then it might help others, and maybe there'll be one less horse sent to slaughter."

Something in her eyes changed while she said the words. She no longer seemed nervous. She wasn't peeking glances at his lips anymore, either. She faced him square on and he knew she'd remembered who he was then and, more important, what he did for a living. He doubted she'd ever let him get close to her again.

Too bad.

SHE HAD HERSELF firmly under control the next morning, or so she told herself. Still, her pulse raced as she pulled into the same parking spot as yesterday. It'd dawned another cool and crisp day, the kind of day that made horses frisky and the scent of fresh-cut grass hang in the air. The sun against the side of the white barn nearly blinded her. She took a deep breath as she emerged from her car, wondering where he was.

"In here," she heard him call.

She headed toward the barn, and the moment she spotted him standing in the middle of the aisle, a friendly smile on his too-handsome face, she knew she'd been kidding herself.

Control. Bah.

"Welcome back," he called.

His black brows lifted when he smiled, and the edges of his eyes crinkled, and it was such a damn friendly smile it made her teeth click and then jam together. Handsome, hunky, hazardous-to-her-health son of a gun.

"Bet your racehorse friends would keel over if they saw me here today."

It was the only thing she could think to say, but it was true. She knew she wasn't liked at the racetrack, and that was okay. As long as she saved horses' lives, that was all that mattered.

"You're probably right, but what they don't know won't hurt them."

In other words, he didn't want it known that she was helping him. The words shouldn't surprise her or bother her, but they did. She tried to hide her disappointment by saying, "Wow. This is nice."

Like the house on the hill, the stable was a showpiece. She'd been so distracted yesterday she hadn't paid much attention, but today she'd noticed that while the outside might be nondescript—a simple whitewashed building with an A-frame roof—the inside was a different story. Old-fashioned open-box stalls stretched down both sides, the kind with three-quarter walls and swooping Regency-style grills atop them. The bars were made out of black iron, higher in the back than in the front, but the change in altitude was accomplished with an almost roller coaster–like curve—very swanky. The face of each stall had the same type of bars, one on the left side and one on the right, gently swooping toward each other and meeting in the middle at the stall door. It was as if she'd been transported back two hundred years—well, except for the rubber mats covering the barn aisle. They even had tack trunks—large wooden boxes that held bits and bridles and maybe even a saddle or two—in between the stalls, although they were covered in red vinyl, the crimson color matching the blankets and halters hanging from the stall fronts.

"Actually, more like amazing," she amended.

"Yeah, my mom had pretty good taste."

He'd just come from the track, and so he wore a red polo shirt with JJJ stitched across the left breast. She could smell the sweat and horses on him and it should have served as a reminder of what it was she was here to do. Instead she found herself simply inhaling the scent of him and then fighting the urge not to close her eyes.

Way to rein in those hormones!

Clearly fifteen hours away from him had done little to cool her jets.

"I like the old-fashioned look of the place," she admitted.

He lifted his cowboy hat, then ran a hand through his ample hair, leaving indented rows where his fingers had touched. "Yeah, although my dad complained the entire time that everything was just fine the way it was." Like a cloud covering the sun, a shadow formed in his eyes. "He never understood the need to show off."

Unlike my mother.

The words were unspoken, but she gleaned what he wanted to say from the tone of his voice.

"You should open up the place for horse boarding." She hoped he picked up on the change of subject, because she didn't like the way staring into his troubled eyes made her heart soften. "I know some hunter/jumper trainers that would kill for a place like this."

"I don't have an arena."

"You could build one. I saw a small track out behind the barn. Build one in the middle."

He tucked his hands in the pockets of his jeans. Alas, that drew her eye to his midsection and what she knew would be a ridge of muscle just beneath his belly button. Did he have hair there, too? Dark hair that formed a V above his…

Stop it!

She couldn't help herself. The man was pure good-looking. He could be the spokesperson for a cologne commercial. Sell whiskey to the Amish. Rocks to a coal miner.

"Unfortunately, that's not in the cards right now."

Because of his finances, she immediately realized. "Maybe if I help you sell one of your horses, you could do it then."

What are you doing?

You shouldn't be helping him to stay in business. Frankly, helping him go *out* of business should be her goal.

His hands slipped from his pockets. He crossed them in front of him. "So you're a veterinarian *and* a horse broker now?"

She shrugged even as inside she mentally sucker punched herself for offering to help him out. *Again.*

"I've come into contact with a lot of different people through vet school, and a lot of really good racehorses are off the track."

He grinned, but it was a small one, the man seeming

almost bemused. "You know, I thought for sure you'd be a real pain in my rear, but you're surprisingly nice."

Aww, how sweet....

She had to swallow back her irritation at herself. "Give it time. I promise to offend you soon."

The smile on his face grew. "You sound like you don't really want to be friends."

"I want to do what's best for the animals."

"It's better than being enemies, though, isn't it?"

No.

She needed him to be an adversary. He was easier to resist that way.

Who was she kidding?

Ever since she'd first spotted him at the racetrack, she'd been smitten. He'd caught her gaze and everything inside her had gone, "Oooh." She'd contained her reaction only by telling herself the man was a jerk—a racehorse owner—so he was ugly inside. Only he wasn't ugly inside. At least, she didn't think so.

She moved toward one of the stalls, berating herself the whole way, but when she caught a glimpse of the animal inside, she said, "Wow."

The dark bay animal took her breath away—huge shoulders, massive hindquarters, long legs, and all topped off with the prettiest head and large brown eyes she'd ever seen. The horse hardly spared her a glance, though; he was napping, back leg resting, ears cocked back casually.

"What a gorgeous animal."

"Yup. He's a dandy, all right," he said with pride. "Dandy of a Dasher, that's his registered name. Dandy for short."

"Is Dandy one of your injured horses?"

He came up next to her and whatever aftershave he wore wafted toward her on a breeze. Sage again. And pine. And then something different, yes, there it was… leather and horses. Her two favorite smells in the world, and they emanated from her enemy.

"He's the one coming off the sesamoid injury."

"How bad of a break was it?"

"Doc called it an apical fracture. No tendon damage. I could probably race him, but…"

If he did, the odds of the horse breaking down again were huge, and the next time might be catastrophic. She clutched the front of the stall, her stomach doing that odd little flip thing again, the same thing it'd done when she'd first spotted him at the track. Most owners would send a horse back to work—damn the long-term consequences. That he didn't, well, it was one more reason to get her lust under control. She could never get involved with a man who raced horses for a living, even if he was one of the nicer ones.

"Did the bone chip?" she asked.

"No. Just a hairline fracture. Enough to make him lame. He's been off since November."

That translated to six months. "He should be nice and healed by now."

"Doc said he is. He gets daily turnout and I haven't seen him take a lame step in months. Just not sure what to do with him."

Okay, brace yourself.

She turned and faced him. "This is exactly the type of horse I think I can help you with." She cleared her throat. "As long as there's no bone chip or full fracture, there isn't any reason why he couldn't go on to perform in a dressage arena or maybe even a jumping pen. I'd want to see his X-rays before I make a judgment call, but if they look good, and you don't mind, I'd like to put some miles on him under saddle, maybe take some new film in a few weeks to see how he's holding up and, if it looks good, call a few friends of mine."

"You want to *ride* him?"

She took a deep breath before facing him again. Why was he looking at her like that? "Yeah. You know. Leg him up, get a feel for what's going on up here." She tapped her head. "Maybe take some video so I can assess how he moves. See if he has any potential."

He'd done it again, moved closer. She hadn't even noticed. "You're really determined to help me, aren't you?"

It felt as if she'd swallowed an air bubble all of a sudden. "Not you," she choked out, "your horses."

"I see. I'm still the enemy?"

She steeled herself. "As long as you race horses, you will always be the enemy."

When she snuck a glance at him, he seemed disappointed and almost hurt.

Ignore it, she told herself.

"Good to know where I stand."

"I just want to make sure we're on the same page."

"Oh, we are."

She nodded. "I'll partner with you, but only for the horses' sake."

"Got it."

She took another deep breath, telling herself she should be grateful he understood.

Why do you feel like such a jerk, then?

"So my first bit of advice is to list your horses on this website I know about. It's for off-the-track racehorses. A lot of trainers keep an eye on what's being posted there."

"Just give me the URL."

"But before we do that, I'll need to ride him first."

"And are you any good at riding?"

She imagined the double entendre to his word. No way was he flirting with her again after what she'd just made clear.

"I grew up on horseback."

"Oh, yeah? Were you one of those spoiled horse-show kids?"

He wasn't being mean, just curious. And, yes, she had definitely imagined the double entendre.

She gave her attention back to the horse. "No. My family couldn't afford riding lessons, so I hung out at the local riding stable. The resident horse expert took pity on me." She tipped her chin up proudly. "It took a lot of hard work, but I learned to ride well enough that I qualified for a national scholarship. Rode for my college team until entering grad school. So, yes, I ride."

"I'm impressed."

Don't fall for his soothing charm.

"If I hadn't learned how to ride, I doubt I would have ever gotten into vet school. We couldn't have afforded it."

When she dared to look into his dark blue eyes again, she saw interest there, maybe even admiration.

"Lucky for all the abused racehorses in the world that you did."

Except his horses didn't look abused. Far from it. Dandy was the picture of good health.

"It's been a while, though," she admitted. "Haven't been on a horse in a few months." She was at the mercy of whoever had a horse that needed exercising since she couldn't afford one of her own, not that she needed one. She had her hands full.

"Why not get back on right now?"

She straightened in surprise. "Oh, I don't know. Dandy's injury..."

"Doc cleared him for work weeks ago."

"Yeah, but I'd still like to look at his chart."

"You don't have to work him. Just walk him around. He'll be fine."

He was challenging her—she could see it in his eyes. Maybe all her talk of being wary adversaries had gotten under his skin. Or maybe he just wanted to see what she was capable of and what he was getting into, not that she blamed him.

"What if he gets away from me in his excitement at being ridden again?" She shook her head. "I'd rather come back tomorrow."

Regroup. Get her head screwed on straight, because right now she had a hard time remembering what he did for a living and that as much as she'd like to succumb to his friendly blue eyes, he could never be her friend.

"Okay, tomorrow it is, but did you want to see the last horse with an injury? It's a filly. No one can figure out what's wrong with her."

"Why don't you get her chart, too?" Because she really just wanted to escape.

He rocked back on his heels, examined her, a hand lifting toward his chin and stroking the razor stubble. "Okay, but she's right over there."

He wasn't going to stop, and it did seem silly to not at least have a look, especially since that was the whole point of her visit this morning. She followed his gaze, spotting a bay filly out in the pasture, an animal as beautiful as Dasher and Dandy.

"What seems to be the problem?"

"Intermittent lameness," he said as they walked to the wooden gate. The thing opened with barely a sound, at least not to her ears, but the filly heard them. She lifted her head.

"I thought at first it was a growth issue, but her joints all look fine. Had her scanned up one side and down the other. A shame, too, because she showed real promise."

Promise as a racehorse. And what better a reminder than the young horse they approached. Beautiful. Sleek. A racehorse. One potentially ruined by him.

"And if I can make her sound again? What then?"

Clearly, he knew the direction of her thoughts. Just as clearly, he didn't want to answer her. "She'll return to work."

"As a racehorse?"

He shrugged.

Well, of course. What did she expect? That he would have a sudden change of heart where racing horses was concerned? Hardly.

The filly turned toward them, nostrils flaring as they approached. Something about their scent must have titillated her senses, because her tail suddenly lifted. Her neck arched. She bolted toward them. If Mariah hadn't known better, the filly would have looked sound, but years of training had taught her to spot the telltale signs of lameness, and she saw it in the horse's gait, especially when she broke into a trot, the filly coming to a halt a few feet away, ears pricked forward, eyes bright.

"Hey there, pretty girl," she heard Zach croon. "How you feelin' today?"

Voice so soft, eyes so kind, hand outstretched as he sought to soothe the fractious filly.

The evil racehorse owner. The horrible horseman. The

man responsible for so many lost lives—equine lives, but just as important to her as human lives.

He cared.

The man took a step closer, whispered soothing words, placed a palm against the horse's neck.

"It's the right front," he said softly.

"I saw that." She approached cautiously. "Has she gotten any better since you put her out to pasture?"

He shook his head as he stroked the animal's mane. "It comes and goes. Sometimes she seems almost sound. Other days—"

Bad. Like today. "And they found nothing on X-rays or scans." Not a question, more of a statement.

"Nothing."

His disappointment had nothing to do with the loss of a valuable racehorse and everything to do with the health of his animal. She knew that, though how she knew it, she couldn't say.

"I'll need to see her chart, too."

He nodded, still petting the horse.

"And perform my own diagnostics."

He faced her again. "Anything you want."

Dear Lord, she didn't want to like the man, but it was hard not to when he stared at her so hopefully.

"I'll do what I can."

"I would appreciate that."

She found herself backing away before she could stop herself, as if he were a dangerous tiger about ready to pounce.

"Call me if you can't get those records. Some clinics can be weird about releasing information."

"I'll let you know."

He moved away from the horse, falling into step next

to her as she hurried toward the exit. The horse followed along, Mariah glancing back in time to spy the limp. Poor thing.

"Thanks for coming out today."

She didn't say anything. She couldn't forget the way he'd studied the filly like a man worried about his best friend. It disturbed her, though not in a bad way.

"Can I take you to lunch? As a way of thanking you?"

"No, no. I, ah, I have another appointment to go to after this."

He didn't say anything, not for the longest time. She saw him scan her face, spotted the way his gaze lingered on her lips, and then his eyes sprouted the faintest hint of a challenge. "Yeah?"

"Yes," she lied.

He knew she didn't have anything more important to do than watch YouTube videos for the rest of the afternoon. Just as he knew she didn't want to spend any more time with him than necessary, and not because of what he did for a living. Oh, no. She didn't want to spend more time with him, because despite what she told herself, she really did like him.

Fool.

There was no denying that she was.

Chapter Five

She hated horse racing.

Zach reminded himself the next morning, and it was all the reason in the world to give Mariah a wide berth. Yet oddly, he kept glancing at his cell phone's clock as he oversaw his morning workouts and then later, on the way back to his ranch.

That cell phone chimed as he turned off the main road. A quick glance revealed what he suspected: email alert. Doc Miller's office. They'd pdf'd the information Mariah needed. When he arrived at his ranch, he headed toward the barn and figured Mariah must already be there, judging by the car parked out front. She had to be in the stall with Dandy because he didn't see her when he glanced down the barn aisle as he headed toward his office. It took him just a moment to print out a black-and-white copy of Dandy's radiographs and the accompanying chart.

Mariah the vet, he thought as he did so. Mariah the champion equestrienne. Mariah the enigma.

She was right where he'd figured she'd be, inside the stall with Dandy tied to an iron bar, an English saddle on his back. She glanced up at him, but it was a quick look, as if she didn't trust herself to make eye contact.

"Hey," he said.

"Hey," she echoed.

He tried to come up with something to say, but all he could think about was how strange it was to have her in his barn. After months of being adversaries it was still hard to wrap his head around Mariah being a friend, not a foe.

"I see you brought your saddle."

She nodded.

"English, huh?"

"No other way to ride." She flipped up the flap of the saddle and buckled the girth.

He almost smiled. "If you say so. Myself, I prefer a Western saddle."

She dropped the flap, eyeing the gelding critically. "Not me."

It was the most mundane conversation in the world, which made him all the more aware of the fact that this was Mariah Stewart in front of him. And she wore breeches and boots. Women in skintight pants and leather boots should be outlawed, he thought, especially women who looked like Mariah. She had the sleek curves of one of his racehorses and the fiery mane of loose hair to match, and he always, *always* noticed even when he told himself not to pay attention.

"Here," he said, thrusting the chart up in the air so she could see it. "All my horses' charts."

She reached through the bars and took the papers from him. He watched as she flipped to the first sheet but only for a moment, her fingers flying to the next sheet and then the next. It was his first chance to observe Mariah the vet in action, and he had to admit, she sure looked like a professional, lips pursing as she paused from time to time. When she got to the radiographs—pdf copies on regular-sized paper—she turned them this way and that, at one point dipping toward the bright end of the barn so she could get a better look. He had no idea if it was the filly's or Dandy's that she studied so intently.

"Dandy's latest scan looks great."

He hadn't realized how tense he was until that moment. "Good."

"Hairline fracture at the most. You can hardly see where it was in the most current film. I doubt it'd even show up in a vet check...as long as he's sound."

"He's sound, but I wouldn't be comfortable selling him to someone who didn't know his history."

She glanced up sharply. "No. Of course not."

"And the filly?"

"Puzzling," she said with a frown at the papers in her hand. "The only thing I can pinpoint are some narrow margins between the coffin bone and the navicular. Most horses have more padding between the two, but it still shouldn't cause her any pain." She looked up at him again. "But you never know. Just like people, some animals are more sensitive than others. I'd want to begin there."

"Great."

She handed him the papers back. "Meanwhile, I'll focus on Dandy."

"If you need a bridle, there's more than a few in the tack room at the end."

"Already grabbed one." She bent and scooped something up. "I assume it's okay to use this one?"

She held up a snaffle bit. A relic of days gone by, back when his mother used to ride, although he noticed she'd cleaned it up some. His mom had been gone from the ranch for nearly a decade, but reminders of her still remained. She'd ridden English, too, but she'd trotted right out of his life the day he'd graduated high school. He sometimes wondered if she'd planned it that way—get him older, then leave.

"The snaffle is fine. That's all we ever work our horses in around here."

"Where can I ride?"

"Out on the track if you like." Memories of his mother were never pleasant.

She slipped the bridle on Dandy, then opened the stall door, and what had looked like a shapely body before suddenly turned into *va-boom.* It was hard to keep his eyes up as she walked by. The woman could be the main act at a men's club. *Shazam.* Just give her a whip and a rope to hang from and she'd be all set, especially with that long red hair of hers hanging down….

"…safety."

He blinked. She stared. He realized she'd asked him a question.

"I'm sorry, what was that?"

She'd spotted him ogling her. He felt his face color for the first time in ages. She narrowed her eyes and suddenly they were back on familiar ground. Protagonist/antagonist, only this time for a whole other reason.

"I asked if you had a helmet."

He nodded. "One of our tack trunks."

He had to hide his chagrin as he turned toward a large wooden box, lifting the chrome lid. Sure enough, an old white skullcap lay inside.

"I don't know if it'll fit." He handed it to her.

She took the thing from him, eyeing the inside skeptically, probably for spiders, before somehow gathering all her hair atop her head and covering it with the helmet.

"It'll do."

She looked nice with her hair tucked away. It accentuated the shape of her face.

Her eyes narrowed.

She'd caught him staring again.

"That type of helmet always reminds me of a gumball." He threw the excuse out, although he half hoped to tease a smile to her lips, though why he bothered he had no idea. It was clear she didn't want to be his "friend" any more than he wanted to be her ally—at least, that was what he told himself.

"How long did you say it's been since he's been ridden?" she asked.

"A while. You sure you're still up for this? We could always have one of my guys get on him first—"

"No need for that."

"Might be safer."

"Don't worry about me."

"Actually, I'm more worried about a lawsuit from your heirs."

She shot him an expression surprisingly full of amusement. "I don't have any heirs, and I would never be the type to sue someone if I fell off a horse, even a racehorse-owning someone."

Her response didn't reassure him. "Maybe I should get on him first."

She pulled Dandy to a stop. "Don't you trust me?"

He smirked. "More like I don't trust my horse."

"He'll be fine." She walked forward again. Dandy followed meekly in her wake.

"Still, I insist I ride him first."

"In an English saddle?"

"Sure. Why not?"

He thought he heard something like a laugh. "You sure you can hang on?"

"Considering I spent my teenage years breezing horses at the racetrack in a saddle no bigger than a tea tray, yes."

She glanced at him with a small smile. Progress.

"Good point."

"Plus, this way you can see how he moves."

They emerged from the barn, the both of them blinking against the late-morning sunshine. In front of them stretched a small racetrack. He'd grown up playing out on that track, had so many good memories connected to the strip of land that it was hard to stomach the idea of maybe one day losing the place.

Don't think that way, he told himself.

She was here because she might be able to help him. If she could, he would owe her, he admitted, not at all sure how that would make him feel.

She opened the gate to the track. He eyed Dandy. Okay, so it'd been a while since he'd been in anything other than a Western saddle.

"Maybe we shouldn't lunge him first," he heard himself say.

"Scared?"

"No." He trusted Dandy. The horse had always been easygoing. He was just being...prudent.

"You want to use my helmet?"

"No need." If he fell and split his head open in front of her, he'd wish he were dead anyway. Still, he pushed his cowboy hat on tighter. "Just go ahead and hold his head while I climb on board."

She did as asked, while Zach eyed the flimsy little

stirrups English riders used. He'd never understood the appeal of such teeny-tiny saddles. When he ponied his horses on the track, he always rode Western. Easier, and the saddles had a horn that he could use to dally a lead rope around if one of his colts got fractious. Still, he'd ridden a large part of his youth bareback; at least he'd have stirrups. He glanced at Dandy. The horse eyed him skeptically—not surprising, since he'd never ridden the animal. Funny how he could own a horse and never ride it.

"Do you want me to get something for you to stand on?"

What? Did she think he was so rusty he'd have a hard time mounting? He didn't know whether to laugh or be offended.

"I'll just swing up."

He grabbed a hank of mane, angled his body in such a way as to achieve maximum velocity, then heaved himself up.

It was hard to say who was more surprised, Dandy or himself—Dandy because Zach had just George-of-the-Jungled into the side of him, not atop him as he had planned, or Zach because instead of landing atop the horse, he'd landed flat on his back on the ground beside him, cowboy hat tipping down and covering his eyes.

"Whoa, whoa, whoa," he heard Mariah murmur to Dandy, trying to soothe him. Hooves danced near his head, then boots, then hooves, Mariah placing herself between him and the upset animal. "Easy there."

Clearly she knew a thing or two about horses, because by the time he sat up, she had things well in hand.

"That was brilliant," he admitted.

He got to his feet. She moved to the side of the horse.

"What are you doing?"

"Getting on."

"Don't do th—"

In the next instant, she'd expertly mounted, the look on her face a cross between bemusement and sympathy.

"If you want, I'll give you a mounting lesson later." But she took the sting out of her words with a smile, the first real one she'd given him in—well, the first one he'd ever had from her. And from nowhere came the thought he'd fall on his face a million times to see that smile.

That troubled him. It troubled him a lot.

Chapter Six

The gelding handled like a dream, Mariah thought a half hour later, another smile coming to her face as she caught sight of Zach.

"You okay?" she asked.

It was hard to look him in the eye and not laugh. The expression on his face when he'd hit the ground… Priceless. She had to work to keep her lips straight all over again. Still, they twitched without her permission.

"More humiliated than anything else," he admitted, lifting his cowboy hat and swiping his hair back. His expression could only be called sheepish and…something else. Something she couldn't quite identify. "Looks like he's behaving for you."

An obvious change of subject. She jumped off Dandy to cover her consternation. Was he surprised that she could actually ride? He seemed a bit perplexed.

"He was, but I'd still like to see him move. Do you mind hopping on? And by that I don't mean *hopping on.*"

She saw him look away, no doubt hiding his embarrassment. He really was being a good sport—hadn't gotten angry, wasn't blustering at her or acting all macho-masculine to make up for falling at her feet. Well, Dandy's feet.

"Sure." He came up to the horse, seeming to hold out his hand to soothe the animal without thought. Dandy didn't move as he climbed aboard as easily as she had. In a matter of seconds he was off and Mariah could tell he could really ride despite his failed attempt at mounting. Within seconds he was trotting. She watched the horse move around her in circles, pleased by what she saw. Actually, pleasantly surprised.

"Okay, bring him in."

"You could tell that quickly?" he asked when he came to a stop in front of her.

"Yup. I could actually tell by the way he walked. He really swings his shoulder. I suspected he would carry himself nicely and he does."

The veins had popped out on Dandy's neck. He'd been worked into a sweat. Still, the animal had a pleasant expression on his face. He was curious about his surroundings but not afraid, and relaxed despite being ridden for the first time in months. "I'll want to work with him for a couple of weeks, but I think he has potential."

Zach's smile was so huge it was all Mariah could do to hold his gaze. Wow.

"Good to hear," he said, patting Dandy again before jumping down. Just as she'd noticed the first day she'd spoken to him, he had a gentle touch. Point in his favor. Actually, he'd gained a lot of points in her book. He'd treated her with respect despite his disdain. He cared for his horses, too. She could tell with every touch.

You like him.

Yes. As much as it was possible to like a man who raced horses for a living.

"So what will you do if he trains up well?" he asked.

"Well, I'll want to ride him for a few weeks and then

call a friend of mine, but I can do that in between overseeing Dasher's therapy. She owns a jumping stable and she's always on the lookout for horses like Dandy."

He touched Dandy's short mane, fiddled with it. "Why?"

"Why what?"

He braced himself before he faced her. She watched as his shoulders became more square, as his mouth tipped into a flat line before he seemed to gather his thoughts.

"Why are you going to so much trouble to help me?"

"Ah," she heard herself say.

"Surely you have better things to do than to help me out. What's in it for you?"

The moment of truth. "What makes you think I want anything?"

He eyed her skeptically. She took a deep breath.

"Okay, fine. I do want something in return."

"And what's that?"

"I want to attend the next owners' meeting." She hadn't meant to blurt the words, but once she said them, she was glad they were out. Too bad he didn't like them.

"I don't think—"

"I know you're on the board at Golden Downs, that you took over your father's seat and that they meet in a couple of days. I was thinking I could go with you." He was going to say no, she could tell. "I'll still work on Dasher and Summer and still ride Dandy for you even if you say no, but if I could talk to the men on the board, convince them to work with me on the best way to dispose of their unwanted racehorses, of everyone's unwanted horses… If we could just get a program in place…"

"I don't think so."

It took an effort not to let her disappointment show. She'd known it was a long shot, but she'd been hoping.

"Could you maybe think about it?"

He nodded, but she could tell he'd probably only think about it for a day and then still tell her no.

Darn it.

She turned to Dandy to hide her disappointment, patted him. Why were these racehorse owners so set in their ways? Couldn't they see there was a problem? Dandy was a classic example of a perfectly wonderful animal going to waste. If she hadn't come along, Zach would have sent him down the road, probably to an auction, and then who knew what might have happened to him?

"We'll get you hooked up with the right person," she told the horse softly.

"I didn't say no."

"You will."

"What do you need me for? You could go on your own."

"And have security called on me the moment they see my face."

"They can't boot you out."

"No, but they can refuse to let me speak."

"They can't do that, either."

"Okay, fine, do you think they'd listen once I open my mouth?"

"And you think I'll lend you some type of credibility?"

"I need an ally, but I can tell you don't want me there, either." She shook her head. "You can't be seen consorting with the enemy, can you? I just hope you think about it for next month's meeting."

"And what if I say yes?"

"But you're not going to."

He lifted a brow.

"Are you?"

He looked past her, then at the ground, then back at her again. "The meeting is the day after tomorrow. That doesn't give you much time to prepare."

"I'll have plenty of time."

She watched as he shook his head. "I'm going to regret this."

She had no conscious thought of moving, but suddenly she'd wrapped him in a hug. "Oh, thank you."

"I haven't said yes yet."

"But it sounds like you're going to, aren't you?"

He sighed. "Yes."

She all but danced in front of him. "I swear to you, Zach, you *won't* regret this."

But *she* already did regret it because when she tried to pull back, he wouldn't let her move. "You have to promise me something."

So blue. Those eyes of his, so amazingly blue. Like the color of the sky on a clear summer morning.

"You have to promise me you'll behave. No shenanigans. No antagonistic T-shirts. No acting like a crazy woman."

"I promise."

Something was happening. Something that robbed her of breath. Something that caused her whole body to buzz and tingle and blush.

Oh, damn.

Time stood still for a moment as everything inside her turned upside down. And then he let her go. It took everything she had to keep standing.

He took the reins from her hands and headed back to the barn without a backward glance.

"Damn," she muttered.

HE SHOULDN'T HAVE DONE IT. He shouldn't have said yes.

A half a dozen times he'd called himself a fool. It wasn't just that he'd agreed to take her to a board meeting that blew his mind. If he was honest with himself, it was what it had felt like to hold her, too, and the temptation to kiss her… Damn. It'd been nearly irresistible. Thank God she'd kept her distance for the next two days. He'd kept his distance, too. The only thing he'd done was text her a time and a place.

He'd been dreading the meeting since she'd pulled away from the ranch after riding Dandy. He'd kept hoping she'd cancel, but he should have known better, and so a half hour before they were due to arrive, he found himself waiting for her near his row of stables. Around him grooms went about the evening chore of feeding, the sky already turned a deep orange. Any minute now the overhead lights would come on. Horses nodded their heads impatiently while they waited to eat, some of them nickering at a favorite human, a few of them banging their knees against the side of the stall in impatience.

"I think I'm going to hyperventilate."

She'd come up behind him, and Zach noted the minute he turned that she appeared ready to vomit.

A wee bit green around the gills? he almost asked.

He bit back a smile. "It's not too late to change your mind."

Lord, he hoped she'd do that. He hadn't told anyone he was going to bring Maddening Mariah. If he had, they'd have told him not to bother. Better to spring it on them, he'd thought. Too late did he begin to wonder what would happen if they told him to get her out.

They wouldn't do that, he reassured himself. Pretty girl like her. She'd piled her hair atop her head in a way he'd never seen before, had left loose curls around her face. She wore a floral-printed loose-fitting tank top, one that hugged her breasts and then fell in soft folds around her waist. Jeans that were tucked into fancy Western boots completed the outfit. His eyes caught on the scalloped pattern before slowly trailing back up her legs, then her midsection and then finally to her eyes.

They blazed.

"Do I meet with your approval?"

"I like you better in T-shirts and jeans."

She looked sexy as hell and after his reaction to her the other day, it made him edgy.

"I do, too." She glanced down. "But I'll do whatever it takes to be taken seriously. None of your brethren has seen me in anything other than jeans and a CEASE shirt. Maybe the change of clothing will help them see me in a new light."

His brethren—as if he were a member of a cult or something.

"Come on."

The meetings were held in the Redondo Room near the Turf Club. It was an easy walk from the stabling area along the short side of the track to the grandstand facilities along the front. Since it was a weekday, the main facility stood empty, but come race day you wouldn't be able to see the bleachers through the people packed into the stands. The opening they crossed through today had no guard, and the pathway they followed was clear of onlookers who usually lined the chain-link fence so they could catch an unimpeded view of the horses on the track. There was another opening farther down, but it led to the parade circle—the place where they circled the horses prerace—and was closed on nonmeet days.

"You know, in all my years of visiting the track, I've never been in the grandstands." She made a face. "Haven't wanted to watch."

"We're really not that bad."

She stopped. "Yes, you are. It's like watching a five-year-old run a marathon."

"Thirteen."

"Excuse me?"

"Research indicates a two-year-old horse is the equivalent of a thirteen-year-old child."

"The point being it's still a child."

"There are plenty of thirteen-year-olds that run track at local meets."

He'd stopped without realizing it, which meant he had a perfect view of her mouth opening and closing. Her cheeks had turned the same shade of shell-pink as the sky above. The lights around the racetrack had popped on.

"Those thirteen-year-olds don't run for a living."

"Damn near. Look at the Olympic gymnasts."

"Those are amateurs."

"Please," he scoffed.

"And they're not kids," she added.

"Hah. Have you seen them? They do backflips at five."

"That's different."

"How?"

"It just is."

Her eyes glared at him like sun off a shard of glass.

"Mariah, you're not going to get very far with the other board members with that kind of thinking."

She looked taken aback for a moment. "But I know I'm right."

"That's your opinion and you better keep it to yourself if you want to make friends."

"With friends like them, who would need enemies?"

"Mariah."

"Okay, okay, I'll be good."

"Promise me?"

"Promise."

He held her gaze, trying to determine if he could trust her. But surely she knew she would get only one shot at convincing the board. She had to tread carefully or they would shut her out, and if that happened, well, there wasn't much he could do for her.

"Come on." He glanced at his cell phone. "We're going to be late."

She swept her hands toward the grandstands. "Lead the way."

How was it possible to be attracted to a woman and yet be so completely exasperated by her at the same time? It made him want to get in her space again, to watch her cheeks bloom with color as he touched her, to just… He ran a hand through his hair. To just get under her skin the way she got under his. Darn woman.

"This way."

Golden Downs had been constructed two decades ago, its white balustrades and spire rooftop reminiscent of Thoroughbred racetracks on the East Coast. They followed a path that led to the base of the stands and a wide corridor beneath the middle of the complex. To their left were stairs and an escalator. To his right were betting windows and an elevator. Only the elevators were working today. He pushed the button.

"It's huge," she said, looking at the wide expanse of concrete and the steel girders overhead.

"Wait until you see the Turf Club."

Years and years ago the spot where Golden Downs had been constructed had been a popular location for match races. With a backdrop of the Santa Ynez Mountains and the ocean only a few miles away, it'd become a popular tourist attraction. After Prohibition, Art Golden, a man better known for his connections to Hollywood, had constructed the raceway. The owners had never looked back. Spring brought quarter horses. Summer meant Thoroughbreds. In the fall they raced harness horses. Never a dull moment at Golden Downs.

"Here we go," he said as the elevator doors opened. It was a short ride for traveling five stories. The whole complex was six stories tall, but he rarely went to the top floor.

The elevator slid open again, revealing a tile lobby flanked on both sides by a wide hallway and double doors directly ahead, the words Golden Downs Turf Club painted in gold lettering on the glass. Two massive flower arrangements sat on either side.

"Nice, huh?" he said, stopping in the middle and eyeing the crown molding and ivory paint scheme. "I'll give you a tour later."

For now he turned left and toward one of several walnut-colored doors set into the same wall as the Turf Club.

The Redondo Room was the last room on the right. It overlooked the stabling area, thanks to windows on two sides. Straight ahead, in front of windows that overlooked the finish line, they'd arranged a row of tables. A few of his fellow board members waved before they spotted who trailed in his wake.

Here we go.

He turned to Mariah and tried to conceal his anxiety. "Sit," he ordered.

"What? Am I a dog?"

His gaze scanned the audience members, of which there were few—the meeting was usually dull as doornails to the general public. "Of course not, but you'll need to sit and be quiet until it's time for you to talk. They'll call for announcements and we'll do it then. I'll tell everyone who you are." He glanced toward the front of the room. "Not that they don't already know."

She muttered, "Really?" in a sarcastic voice as he headed to his seat.

Wesley Landon, one of his closest friends, shot him a brow à la Spock as he sat down next to him.

"Is that who I think it is?" he asked.

The door opened as the last two board members headed for the front of the room.

"It is." Zach scanned the agenda in front of him. The usual stuff: reading of the minutes, changes to race dates, disciplinary actions.

"You brought Mariah Stewart to a board meeting?" He could hear amusement in Wes's voice. "Are you *nuts?*"

Whatever he might have said was interrupted by Edward Golden, grandson of Arthur Golden, when he said, "Are we ready?"

Everyone nodded.

As he'd told her the other day, anyone could attend the meeting, even someone as reviled as Mariah. Still, Zach jumped when Edward pounded the table with a wooden hammer and brought the meeting to order.

He barely heard the rest of what was said; he fiddled with his brass nameplate, shuffled through the agenda the secretary had printed out. Clicked a pen on and off. Try as he might, he couldn't shake the fear that she'd stand up and shout something controversial. She didn't. Instead she seemed to be content to study the other board members, no doubt painting villainous mustaches on them all. There wasn't much to see. A mix of young men and old. Some had been on the board for decades. Others, like Wesley and him, were relatively new, although he might lose his seat after bringing Mariah to the meeting.

An hour ticked down. His stomach churned like a riptide just before he heard the words he'd been dreading.

"Any announcements?" asked Edward.

It wasn't too late to back out, he told himself. He could keep quiet. But instead he lifted his hand. "Actually, yes."

All eyes turned. Nearly everyone had seen Mariah walk in with him, and if there'd been any doubts that they were together and that his "announcement" had to do with her, they'd have been banished the moment he motioned her forward.

"I invited an…acquaintance of mine to speak tonight."

Edward wasted no time. "Whatever she has to say can be submitted to the board and put on next month's agenda." The man hardly spared him a glance. "Anybody else have an announcement?"

He should have felt relief. He was off the hook. And just as she'd predicted, they weren't going to give her any time to talk. He should have just let it go. Instead he heard himself say, "Wait, wait, wait."

Everyone stared in his direction.

He swallowed. "Ms. Stewart has something to say and I think we should let her speak."

"Next month."

He met Mariah's gaze, shook his head gently, trying to silently apologize. They'd try again next month, he told her with his eyes.

She bolted upright. "There's no reason for me to return next month." Those sitting in the front row jerked around. "What I have to say won't take long."

"Mariah—"

"It will just take a minute."

She wasn't going to listen to him. Instead she shuffled sideways to exit her row. "Just hear me out." She didn't approach the head table, just paused in the middle of the aisle, glancing at each of his fellow board members, and said the words he should have expected. Should have, but hadn't.

"I want you to stop racing horses."

Chapter Seven

This was her moment, Mariah told herself firmly. Too bad Zach was staring at her as though he wished the floor would open up and swallow her whole.

"Excuse me?" she heard someone say.

She scanned faces in an attempt to spot who had spoken, but her gaze hooked on Zach instead. She tried to appear apologetic, but she had only a moment to reflect on the disappointment in his eyes before turning to the man in charge of the meeting—Edward Golden, according to his nameplate—who waved his hammer at her as if he might toss it in her direction like Thor.

"Who do you think you are to demand such a thing?" he asked.

"A concerned citizen."

"Lady," said another man, George Lohan, she noted, a man with gray hair and skin so dark it nearly matched the finish of the furniture. "You clearly have some misconceptions about the racing industry."

Why did they always *say* that? She contained her impatience only by counting to ten.

"Believe me, sir, I understand completely what it is you do with your animals. I'm a veterinarian." She tipped her chin up proudly, but the men in the room shot her looks of skepticism. "No. I am. I've spent the last few years gelding stallions in Third-World countries."

"Excellent," exclaimed Edward Golden. "You should go back to doing exactly that."

"Not until I finish my work here."

"Young lady, there *is* no work for you to do here," the owner of the track said in as snide a voice as she'd ever heard. "Men have been racing horses for centuries. We don't need a woman to tell us what to do."

She realized in that instant that she would never get through to him, to all of them. They might listen to what she had to say, but only because they couldn't exactly throw her out. But maybe…

"Gentlemen," she said, softening her voice and glancing at Zach for a moment. The man wouldn't even look her in the eye. Well, fine, she'd do this without him. She moved forward, hoping against hope they could see the sincerity in her gaze or, failing that, hear it in her voice. "I know I've caused you some trouble in the past."

The man with blond hair and green eyes sitting next to Zach—Wesley Landon, said his brass plaque—released something close to a snort, but he smiled when he caught her eye, even nodded to her in encouragement. She felt her shoulders sag. At least she had one ally.

She took a deep breath. "I realize I'm probably fighting a losing battle, but I have to try." She had all of their attention now. Even the scoffing one, Edward, the only one in the room she'd had direct contact with in the past, and it hadn't been good, so she'd expected that. "Hundreds of horses a year are sent to slaughter because of the overbreeding of racehorses. I realize your organization isn't to blame for all of the animals, but you're part of the problem. If you could just take a stand. Stop racing, even if it's just for a few months, long enough for your horses to mature some more. If you did that, you'd give them a better chance at reaching maturity without serious injury. They could go on to other careers when you're finished with them—"

"Do you have any other suggestions?" Mr. Golden asked in a tone of voice that indicated he wouldn't care if she offered to buy every horse on the racetrack in order to save their lives.

"This is the only solution."

"Duly noted." Mr. Golden looked around the room. "Any other announcements?"

"Wait a minute. You need to hear me out."

"With all due respect, Miss Stewart, we don't have to do anything."

"But you're killing horses."

"Are we?" Mr. Golden scoffed. "Forgive me, but I don't recall having to put a horse down."

"No, of course not. You send them someplace else to be killed."

"Hogwash."

"You might as well pull the trigger—"

"That's enough," Mr. Golden said.

"You may return to your seat, Miss Stewart."

She almost didn't. The heat of rebellion stirred in her chest. She wanted to storm up to Edward Golden and tell him she would be back, that he could count on it and that he couldn't keep on ignoring the problem. Instead she swallowed back her anger and her pride and reluctantly turned away, but not before she caught a glimpse of Zach's face, and the look in his eyes nearly made her stumble. He stared at her like a man who'd been brought to disappointment by a good friend.

She realized then that she'd alienated the one person in the room who might have been in a position to help her.

Damn.

"ZACH." SHE CALLED OUT his name from behind him, and Zach quickened his steps as he headed toward the bank of elevators, his footfalls echoing on the marble floor.

"Fine. Ignore me. But you won't be able to ignore me tomorrow when I come out to work with Dandy."

He pushed the button for the elevator and wouldn't you know it, the damn thing wasn't waiting. Never failed. When you wanted to leave quickly, you always had to wait.

"Zach."

She pushed herself in front of him.

He didn't want to look at her. If he did, she would see how upset she'd made him. So he clenched his jaw and turned away.

"I'm sorry."

Behind him he heard someone else leave the meeting and the last thing he wanted or needed was for anyone to think there was more between the two of them than there really was. He had a feeling he'd be in more hot water than he already was.

She touched him.

He swung away. "Let's talk," he said, leading her toward the Turf Club doors. They were open, thankfully, though the place was deserted. He saw the reason the door had been left open when they passed a door to their immediate left. Glenda, the events coordinator for Golden Downs, sat at her desk, her short gray hair as meticulously in place as it always was.

"Hey, Glenda."

The events coordinator looked up, the frown on her face fading when she saw it was him.

"Zach. Hey." She placed a piece of paper she'd been reading back on her desk. "Board meeting over?"

He nodded at the older woman. "Mind if we sit and chat a spell?" He motioned with his chin toward Mariah.

Glenda had known him since he was in diapers. She'd been running things upstairs for as long as Zach could remember, and with opening night the next day, he wasn't surprised she was working late.

"No. Go ahead." She waved toward the windows and the wooden tables placed in front of them. "Looks like I'll be here awhile."

She went back to work before he could say thanks. Zach led Mariah to the farthest corner of the room. The place always reminded him of a casino, right down to the brass railings that separated the upper level from the lower. Canned lighting and a diamond pattern on the carpet only added to the feeling. It was dark outside now, but the track beyond had been lit for evening workouts. The massive fixtures overhead shone light down on the dark brown footing, making it as bright as day. A lone horse galloped on the track, its rider gingerly perched atop the animal's back, the horse's head bobbing in rhythm to its stride. The track must have been recently groomed, because that horse left a trail of hoofprints in its wake.

"It's beautiful up here," she said.

Why did he have the feeling she would have never complimented anything about the racetrack if she weren't so worried about his obvious anger?

"Is it?"

"Look at that view." Below, the track spread out in front of them, another horse and rider just entering the track, the animal's trainer going up to and then leaning against the rail. "I've only ever seen this in pictures."

When he followed her gaze, he spotted their reflections in the glass, Zach leaning back and unable to keep the displeasure from his voice as he said, "Yup. Down below is where we denizens of moral corruption ply our trade. Look. There's another one right there." He pointed.

She couldn't hide her chagrin. "Okay, so I might have come on a little too strong."

"You think?" The tables inside the club were covered in white linen, bread plates on top of them and empty water goblets, too. He toyed with an empty glass. "But I don't know. Maybe calling me and other horse owners murderers is an effective way to curry support."

Her lower lip jutted out as she contemplated her response. Down below, the new arrival on horseback began to trot in their direction.

"I knew it was a long shot." She met his gaze as the rider on the track increased his speed. "And that the proverbial odds were stacked against me, but I was hoping they would at least listen."

"Maybe they would have if you hadn't been so damn offensive."

She winced. "Okay, I deserved that."

"I told you to be polite."

"I *was* polite."

"Hah."

"If you knew what I really wanted to say to your friends, you'd be horrified."

He shook his head. "Nothing you say could surprise me."

"I promise, next time I'll be good."

"Next time?"

"I need to come up with a plan. Something they can't say no to." She faced him again. "Maybe a digital presentation. Invite the media—"

"No."

Her chin popped up. "They'll have to listen to me if the media is around."

"No. The old-timers will feel backed into a corner. Not a good thing."

"So what should I do?"

"I don't know, but I'm not going to stick my neck out for you again, that's for sure."

She snorted. "Meanwhile, more horses will be sent to the track and injured and more horses will die."

"Rome wasn't built in a day."

But she wasn't paying attention to him. He followed her gaze. A poster hung on the wall, an advertisement.

"Oh, no."

"Tomorrow is the first day of the spring meet," she mused.

"You're not crashing the opening-day party."

"Why can't I?"

"Because security will toss you out."

"It's open to the public, too."

"Yeah, but nobody has to listen to your speeches. They'll boot you out if you raise a ruckus."

"What about you? Won't you be there? You could run interference."

"I'm not bringing you. I'm in enough hot water as it is. You shouldn't go, either. You've already stepped on enough toes to keep a podiatrist in business for a year. Showing up tomorrow will only pour salt in the wounds."

She stood up slowly. "I should get going."

"Mariah, don't." He stepped in front of her.

"You don't get it, do you?" She glared at him. "This is important to me."

"Believe me, after the stunt you just pulled in there—" he jerked a thumb in the direction of the boardroom "—I get it."

"Then you should know I'll do whatever it takes to be heard, including crash a party."

"Mariah, convincing us to stop racing horses is never going to happen." He moved in closer, and as always happened whenever she was near, he became aware of her body, her heat. "Racing is what we do for a living. It's our life. You're asking us to give up our livelihood."

"Wait. Do you have a horse running tomorrow?"

Why didn't he want to answer her? "I do."

She held his gaze for so long, and he suddenly felt like the one who should be blushing. "Oh."

That was all she said, that one word, but there was a wealth of disappointment in it. And sadness. And, yes, even a touch of resignation—and it stung.

"Look. I can't stop you from going tomorrow. The Turf Club is open to the public, but if you do go, can I give you some advice?"

She didn't answer.

He plunged on anyway. "Focus on an item you can change, like, I don't know, forming a welfare league or something."

She didn't answer and with each passing moment he became convinced she would do exactly as she pleased. When she started to shake her head, he knew he was right.

"I like you, Zach, I really do, even if I don't like what you do for a living. And I promise, I'll continue to help you with your horses no matter what, but I cannot sit back and watch you and your friends run horses into the ground, not without taking a stand."

It shocked him how much her words hurt him, how much it wounded him to be lumped in with the people she hated so much.

"And what about the horses you're helping me to heal? What about them? What if Dasher makes it back to the track?"

"You're not going to race Dasher again, are you?"

"I was thinking I might."

"Don't."

"What if he completely recovers?"

"He won't. He'll always have scar tissue that might pose a problem later."

"Okay, okay, I won't race him, but what about Summer? What if she gets better?"

She nodded sharply. "I know you'll do what's right."

She doesn't dislike *you. You heard her.*

It was little consolation.

"You're going to do this no matter what I say, aren't you?"

"I am."

It was his turn to shake his head. "Don't make a big scene."

"I won't."

"Try to be reasonable."

"I will."

He turned away before he did something truly stupid, like let her see how much her accusations stung. Racing horses was who he was. It was his life. He had no idea why her aversion to his livelihood hurt so much or why it even mattered.

He just knew it did.

Chapter Eight

She'd hurt him.

She watched as he left the Turf Club, leaving her to find her own way back to her car.

Who was she kidding? He'd almost run away from her.

As she rode the elevator down to the mezzanine, she admitted he had a right to be angry. He was helping her and she'd completely ignored his advice. She might be helping him out in return, but that didn't mean she should abuse his trust. She owed him an apology. Maybe even dinner. Something.

As it turned out, she didn't have time to give it much more thought. A local veterinary clinic called and asked if she could assist in an emergency surgery. She jumped at the chance but ended up spending most of the night and the early-morning hours helping to keep an eye on the sick horse. Then she fell into bed, nearly missing the alarm she'd set. When she finally managed to open her eyelids, she wanted only to close them again.

"You up in there?" someone called.

Mariah sat up in bed.

"We're all starting to worry about you out here."

Jillian Thacker, her best friend and a woman who

didn't know the meaning of the word *no.* She'd keep banging until Mariah opened up the door.

"I'm coming," she called. "Just a minute."

She'd passed out in her scrubs, never a good thing considering all the crud she tended to collect on the front. With a grimace of distaste she pulled off the matching olive-green pants and shirt. She was still in her jeans and fancy shirt from the evening before. Still presentable. Well, aside from the messy hair. Sometime during the night it had come down.

"What took you so long?" Jillian asked the moment Mariah opened the door, her black bob gliding over cheeks as high as the Alps. Bright green eyes lit up with a smile when she spotted her. "It's hotter than rocket fuel out there."

Was it? Mariah glanced outside, squinting against the brilliant afternoon sun. She lived on a boarding ranch. Free rent in exchange for free veterinary care of the owner's show horses. It worked out because she frequently practiced medicine on more than the owner's horses. The facility's clientele was the kind that loved having their own resident vet on the premises. She'd made a lot of good friends over the past year, including Jillian. She hadn't been kidding when she'd told Zach she had connections in the horse world.

"Nice and cool inside," she said, closing the door behind her.

"Is that what had you sleeping so late?"

It was a tiny studio apartment. Bathroom to her right, futon to the left, kitchen in the back.

Mariah sighed. "Colic surgery last night. I was asked to assist Dr. Baffert. Took us forever to get the horse sedated, and then we couldn't find the impaction, and then the good doctor asked me to close for him while he went back to bed, I presume. I was there until five this morning.

"Gee. No wonder you look like hell."

Jillian might be five feet nothing, but she was a spitfire. Given what she did for a living, that wasn't surprising. Animal communicator, that was her official title, and it caused a fair amount of grief. Mariah had been a skeptic herself when she'd first moved into Uptown Farms, but a persistent lameness had convinced her. Mariah hadn't been able to diagnose the horse. No vet had been able to do so. Jillian had told her it was the horse's shoulder. When Mariah had asked what made her think that, Jillian had admitted the horse had told her. A body scan had revealed a torn meniscus. Problem solved. Over the past year she'd made a believer out of Mariah. In fact, maybe it wouldn't hurt to have her "read" Zach's filly.

"All I want to do is go back to bed."

"Then do it. We were just worried about you, is all."

"We" were the other boarders who came and went during the day. Uptown Farms was Grand Central Station at times, people constantly coming and going. The head trainer, Natalie Goodman, was in demand. She and her clients liked to keep an eye on the newly minted vet, as they liked to call her, inviting her to ride from time to time.

"Believe me, I would love to go back to bed."

"Why can't you?" Jillian wiped a strand of black hair off her face. She liked it longer in the front than in the back. A lot of people wouldn't be able to carry such a haircut off, but Jillian looked like a fashion model with her catlike cheekbones and wide lips.

"I have to go out tonight."

Jillian's bright green eyes lit up like a marquee sign. "A date?"

"Hardly." She sighed. "Opening day at Golden Downs."

Those same eyes narrowed. "More protesting?"

"Actually, I'm going to crash the Turf Club."

Silence. She saw Jillian's eyes scan her face, as if she were hoping to read her human friend's mind. "You're going to the Turf Club?" She clucked her tongue.

"It's not what you think."

"You're not going to create a big scene? Or orchestrate an impromptu video presentation? Or stand up on a table and give a speech?"

"Actually, all I want to do is speak to Edward Golden, chairman of the board at Golden Downs."

"I know who he is."

"I think I need to work things from a different angle."

She turned toward her closet—an antique armoire—near the back of her apartment. It was blocked by Jillian.

"Mariah, what's going on?" Blue eyes bored into her own. "This wouldn't have anything to do with that horse-trainer guy, would it?"

She had nothing to hide, Mariah reminded herself. So what if Zach's look of disappointment had pricked at her conscience. He knew how she felt about horse racing, just as she knew what he did for a living. Any semblance of a friendship they had formed this week was just temporary. She needed him and he needed her. That was all.

"Mariah?"

Jillian was still waiting for an answer, she realized. "Nothing's going on, if that's what you mean." She tried to brush past her friend.

"Oh, no, you don't. It's that guy, isn't it? That Zach guy. You've been seduced by the dark side, haven't you?"

"Don't be ridiculous." This time her friend let her pass, Mariah resisting the urge to dive into the oversize cabinet and close the door. At least she'd escape from the heat of Jillian's gaze.

"I've seen his picture." She heard Jillian behind her. "The man's a bona fide hottie."

"I should wear something businesslike," Mariah muttered. "He needs to take me seriously. Last night I looked too…flower child."

"Oh, please." Jillian crossed her arms in front of her, moving to stand by one of the open doors of the closet. "What you really want is to wear that sexy black number that hugs your curves and shows off your legs."

"No, I don't."

But if she wore that black dress, it sure would knock the uptight man on his ass. She'd knock them all for a loop. Wouldn't that be something? Especially Zach—

She stepped back.

"See!"

She whirled to face Jillian. "Stop."

But she lied to herself. She did like Zach. He'd been nothing but sweet and helpful and considerate and she'd betrayed his trust and thrown what he did for a living in his face.

"See!" Jillian pronounced again.

Thankfully, her kitchen table wasn't too far away; otherwise she might have sunk to the floor.

"I *do* like him." It sounded like a death-bed confession even to her own ears. She jerked her head up, meeting Jillian's gaze. "But that's not why I want to wear that dress."

The table and chairs were a relic from the '60s. Metal legs scraped against a linoleum floor as Jillian pulled a chair out. "Spill."

She found herself shaking her head. "He's nothing like I expected."

"Zach?"

She crossed her arms in front of her. "He's sweet."

"Uh-oh."

"Don't 'uh-oh' me."

Her friend leaned back, her small chin dropping down low. "Look. I understand why you're helping him. We all understand that. Those bastards have no idea how much stress they put on their horses and you're in a position to help one or two of them." She leaned in closer. "But to actually like the man responsible for doing that to a horse. Have you lost your mind?"

"No," Mariah said. "I mean, I know Zach races horses for a living, but he has this gelding named Dandy that injured its sesamoid. He could have put him back into training after it healed, but he didn't. He retired him. I'm going to talk to Natalie about him. See if maybe he might work as a hunter-jumper prospect."

"Oh, man. You're into him big-time."

"I want to help his horses."

"A week ago you wanted to shut guys like him down."

She couldn't deny it. She wasn't even going to try. "My meeting last night didn't go very well."

"Did they toss you out?"

"Not quite," she admitted, getting up from the chair, surprised to note she was sore from her night of squatting down by a sick horse's side. It came with the territory, though. "Afterward Zach reminded me that you can catch more flies with honey."

Jillian didn't say anything. Mariah almost dreaded facing her again, and when she did, she wasn't surprised at the look of dismay on her friend's face. "I never would have thought you'd turn rogue."

"Jillian, I haven't turned rogue." But she sounded like she tried a little too hard to convince herself. "I just think he has a point, especially after the disastrous meeting I had last night. They refused to listen. They won't *ever* listen if I keep being confrontational." She plopped down on the chair again. "Zach is right. CEASE has staged protests and lockouts and enlisted the aid of the media, none of which has done a darn bit of good. So I decided to do as Zach suggests. I'm going to propose CEASE help form an animal-welfare alliance. A group of concerned individuals made up of CEASE participants and members of the racing community who could generate ideas on how best to help unwanted racehorses, you know?"

Jillian eyed her skeptically.

"Let me guess. One member of the racing community will be Zach?"

"No, not just him. Others, too...hopefully. I'm going to work from the inside out. Get close to the people who matter."

"Including Zach."

She flung herself up and returned to the wardrobe. "Will you stop with that?"

"I'm just sayin'."

She knew what she was saying, but it wasn't true. She liked Zach. After last night and her reaction to the disappointment she'd spotted in his eyes, she could no longer deny it. That didn't mean she was going to get close to him. No way. No how. Not unless he stopped racing horses.

"I'm just going tonight to speak to Mr. Golden. This has nothing to do with Zach."

"If you say so."

And she was going to wear that dress, she thought,

pulling the thing out of the closet, but it was only to throw the men on the board off guard.

That was what she told herself.

Because she would apologize to Zach, too. It was the least she could do.

SHE'D SENT HIM a text that she'd like to see him.

Zach hadn't expected that.

He'd assumed she'd just show up at the Turf Club and he'd maybe bump into her. Truth was, race days were chaotic. Since he was an owner *and* a trainer, it meant sticking by his horse's side until the last possible moment and then heading up to the owners' box. A side trip to the Turf Club beforehand would make things more difficult.

Still, when he got her text, he found himself thinking he actually had time to meet her until he abruptly told himself to knock it off. He'd see her tomorrow, at his farm.

She hated racing.

No, he silently amended, watching as one of his grooms wrapped his horse's front legs, she hated what he did for a living. She didn't hate *him.* She'd made that clear last night.

But as he went about his race-day preparations, he found himself glancing at his cell phone. He hadn't responded, probably wouldn't have, either, except fifteen minutes before he was due to meet her he received a one-word text.

Please?

Damn it.

He shouldn't. He really shouldn't. He should just leave her hanging.

"Listen, Jose, I'm going to make a quick trip up to the Turf Club. I have to meet a..." He searched for the right word. "A potential client. I'll be back in time to saddle."

"Okay, boss," the man said, hardly sparing him a glance.

His horse would be in good hands. His staff knew the drill. They'd never let him down. Frankly, Zach's job was done as of race day. If he didn't have his horse in top physical shape by now, it was too late. Race day was nothing more than a waiting game. Still, he had his little ritual. Arrive early. Feed the horses. Reroll bandages. Check tack. He liked to keep to his routine. So why was he rushing off to meet Mariah?

Beat the hell out of him.

Today bodies were packed into every crevice, forcing him to use a private entrance. A security guard barely looked his way as he headed through the owner/trainer gate that took him around the race-day crowd. They even had their own exclusive elevator.

He could hear the murmur of voices before the elevator door opened. The private elevator car stopped and Zach could see the double doors to the Turf Club were wide open. The maître d' stationed at the entrance nodded a greeting as Zach passed by and he wondered how he'd ever find Mariah in the crush of bodies.

He didn't have far to look.

Honestly, he would have spotted the mass of gorgeous red curls two hundred yards away—she'd left her hair long and loose and it shone like a molten waterfall—but it was the crowd of men around her that caught his eye, or rather their laughter. All right, it was the backless dress she wore, too. He'd always been a sucker for a sculpted back, and Mariah's had twin ridges on either side of the spine, her skin as flawless as her face.

Whatever she'd said to the group of horse owners, most of whom he knew only by sight, not name, it'd made them all laugh again. One of them, a second-generation owner not much older than him, placed a hand on her shoulder.

Zach moved forward so quickly he nearly ran over a waiter carrying a tray of champagne.

"Sorry," he muttered.

By the time he came up behind her, Mariah had adroitly shifted away from the man touching her, which immediately lowered Zach's tension level.

And why is that? asked a voice.

He knew why. He just didn't want to *admit* to knowing why.

"...and then the owner said to Jillian, 'Well, how do I know you're telling me the truth?' And my friend says, 'Well, Houdini also told me he doesn't like the brown-haired woman you bring to the barn at night. She makes too much noise. He wants you to know he likes the blonde woman much better,' and then my friend Jillian points to the man's wife, who's standing at her husband's side with a look of horror on her face."

The men surrounding Mariah stared at her, their eyes widening.

"You mean," said the young owner, a man Zach remembered was Brett Vandicott, "the man's horse outed him to his wife?"

"Yup," Mariah said. "Right in front of said wife."

"Incredible," said an owner old enough to be Mariah's father but who stared at her in frank interest nonetheless. "Are you sure your friend Jillian didn't hear a rumor?"

"Positive. She had no clue who the man was before she'd met him. She's the real deal."

Mariah glanced around as if she was looking for someone.

Him?

She must have caught him standing there out of the corner of her eye, because she turned and he could have sworn her eyes lit up, but only for a millisecond because then she smiled. "You made it."

If the back of her was stunning, the front of her took his breath away. She wore makeup, and while she didn't need it, whatever she'd done to her eyes made them huge. It turned the brown nearly green and completely mesmerized not just him but everyone around her. With her hair down, the halter neck of that dress exposing alabaster shoulders, and her eyes luminous and large, she looked, in a word, *stunning.*

"Per your request."

"I'm glad." She sent an apologetic smile to the group at large. "Got to go, gentlemen."

"Wait. You can't go running off with her now." Brett's smile was the epitome of an open invitation, one that projected how much he'd like her phone number. "We're just getting to know her."

By *we,* he actually meant *he,* something that set Zach's teeth sliding into one another even though it didn't matter to him one iota if she hooked up with the man.

Or so he told himself.

"Actually," Zach said, "you've met Mariah before. You probably just don't recognize her without her protest signs."

Silence. A couple of the men glanced between Brett

and Mariah. One of them, the old man, asked, "Protest signs?"

"Yeah." Zach placed an arm around Mariah's bare shoulders. "Didn't you know? Mariah here is our resident animal-rights activist. The one who likes to stop traffic with her creative posters like Save a Racehorse—Shoot Its Owner."

Beneath his hand, her warm shoulders tensed. The men around all stared at him in disbelief until one of them pointed and said, "You're the one that founded CEASE?"

One glance at Mariah's face and Zach knew she was livid, absolutely red-faced livid, but damn it all, she'd insulted him last night, had all but admitted to despising racehorse owners—oh, wait, everyone but him—and now here she was making nice to a group of those same owners.

"The one and only," Zach answered for her.

She shot him a look that was as disappointed as he'd felt yesterday. "But tonight I'm not here about that." She smiled at the five men around her. "Tonight I'm here as a goodwill ambassador. I'm turning over a new leaf. Taking another approach. Joining the party, so to speak."

It was the right thing to say, because the men smiled back. Of course, she was so dang gorgeous, what else were they gonna do?

"Nice meeting you gentlemen." Mariah flashed Zach a smile as fake as the teeth in the old man's mouth. "Ready?"

He turned away with his own fake smile.

She'd stopped by one of the brass railings, the room so crowded he could smell the sweet scent of her perfume or body lotion or whatever it was she wore, but when she turned to face him, he knew he'd pushed her too far.

"And to think—I actually asked you here to apologize."

The words were hard to hear over the sound of clinking glasses and the murmur of voices. Through hidden speakers the piped-in voice of Pete Smith, the track's announcer, came through. He informed everyone that the horses were coming out of the infield tunnel and suddenly the room became a flurry of activity as people headed toward their tables.

"I was just giving them a heads-up. You know, in case they were thinking you might actually be interested in what they do for a living."

Okay, so now that they were away from the group of men, he felt a little bit bad.

"You didn't have to make me sound like a crazy person," she all but growled.

"I thought you were here to schmooze the board of directors."

When he glanced down at her, he was just in time to see her peek out the row of windows to her right. Outside, beneath a cloudless blue sky, the horses had begun to parade onto the track. She turned away quickly.

"I'm here to make the best of things," she said. "When I got here early, I thought why not try and make friends with a couple of the other horse owners. You know, maybe they'd let me re-home some of their horses, too."

"Brett wanted you in his home, all right, or more accurately, in his bed."

She looked as if he'd slapped her. "I would never trade sex for favors."

No. Of course not. He knew that firsthand. What was more, it'd been a good idea to get to know some of the other owners. Damn it. What was wrong with him? Sure, he'd started off wanting to get under her skin, but now he didn't know what he wanted.

"I know," he admitted.

She glared.

"And I appreciate you wanting to apologize."

She lifted a brow.

"I'm sorry, too."

Finally, she softened her gaze. She tipped her chin up, though, as if daring him to continue.

"I shouldn't have outed you like that," he conceded.

"Apology accepted."

He inhaled, trying to figure out what was wrong with him. Maybe it was that dress. He'd felt funny since the moment he'd spotted her there. It was almost as if he couldn't catch his breath.

"It's just that Brett Vandicott is the biggest jerk that ever walked the earth. He'd pretend to listen to what you have to say just to get you into his bed."

"I can handle myself around men like him."

She probably could. "Just the same, you're better off focusing your efforts on me and the board."

Me and the board?

Why had he lumped himself in with everyone else? He really had very little power. It was Edward Golden she needed to impress.

She didn't seem to notice his words, though. She was too busy watching a nearby TV screen and judging by the look on her face, she'd caught sight of the horses out on the track, her eyes quickly darting away. He saw despair in that gaze before she looked away.

"You're right. I should try and speak with him as soon as possible." She met his gaze again. "I just wanted to say I'm sorry to you first. You've been kind to me, Zach. And you're a good man. I wanted you to know that. Wanted you to know that *I* know that."

And then she moved forward, tipping up on her toes to kiss him on the cheek.

"Wish me luck."

She turned to leave, and before he could stop himself, he heard himself say, "Wait."

She abruptly faced him again and he spotted it then, the fear, the anxiety, the glimmer of—what was it, hope? Yes, he admitted. Hope that he might do something nice all over again—like confront Edward Golden with her.

Damn.

"If you want, I could go with you."

What is wrong *with you?*

He liked her. He liked her passion. He liked how committed she was to the animals she loved. He loved them, too. He just needed to prove to her how much.

"Zach, you don't have to."

"I know, but there's less chance he'll be rude if I'm by your side."

She grabbed his hand, just briefly, and Zach knew he was sunk when his gut fluttered almost as if he were about to get on a frightening amusement park ride.

"Thank you," she said.

"No problem."

But she was a problem. A huge problem. He'd only begun to realize just how big.

Chapter Nine

She'd kissed him! And touched him! Had she lost her mind?

It was her nerves, she told herself. She wasn't thinking straight. She should have never asked him up to the Turf Club. Except…except…she was glad he was here.

"We better hurry," he said. "The race is about to start."

The race. The horrible horse race. *Zach* raced horses. She shouldn't want him by her side. But when he stopped near a table belonging to Edward Golden, she was so very grateful that he'd volunteered to go with her.

"Edward," Zach said.

Edward looked up with a smile, the grin freezing on his face when he spotted who it was and, more important, who stood beside him. "Zach." He inclined his head in greeting, ignoring her.

"Why, hello, Mr. Golden," she said with a warm smile. "Good to see you again."

The man appeared not to have heard her.

"You remember Mariah from the meeting, don't you?"

The man did, he just didn't want to admit it. He glanced at the track, ostensibly to follow the progress of his colt, Mariah guessed, but probably more as a way to gather his words and compose himself before turning to face her again. She knew he didn't like her. That should have filled her with satisfaction. Oddly, it didn't.

She took a deep breath, used every ounce of her will-power to paste a contrite expression on her face and tried to project friendliness when she said, "Of course he remembers me."

When he met her gaze, Mariah had a hard time maintaining the facade. Wow. He didn't just dislike her. He loathed her.

She realized in that instant that she would never, ever, not in a million years, convince the man to suspend racing two-year-olds. She'd have a better shot at getting him to race cows.

"I'll bet I'm on a very short list of the top ten people he most despises," she admitted. "And I don't blame him after the way I've behaved."

Okay. It was a lie. She wouldn't take back anything she'd done to forward her purpose. Not a single thing, but she must have hid it well, because Edward's gaze grew a little less hostile. Not so the women at his table. When Mariah included them in her smile, she received the equivalent of cat claws, one of the women going so far as to turn her back. The other woman grabbed the arm of the man next to her—it must have been her husband—and pointed at something out on the track. They both looked away.

Whatever.

She wasn't some pampered princess turning a blind eye to what was going on, unlike the people in this room. She held her head high despite the cold shoulder launched in her direction.

"Mr. Golden, if I could have a moment of your time."

Reluctantly, it seemed, the man turned his attention to her again.

She took another deep breath. "I know I've been a thorn in your side and I'm sorry for that, but I want you to know that I've turned over a new leaf."

"Really?"

She didn't hesitate before saying, "Yes. Zach here has helped me see the wisdom of forming an animal-welfare league peopled by both racing insiders and animal-welfare specialists." She glanced up at Zach, silently thanking him for the idea. "I am hoping, truly hoping, that we can put the past aside and look forward to a future of mutual respect."

She could have sworn Zach moved in closer, not a lot but enough that she felt his presence. It helped to bolster her bravado, especially when Edward didn't say anything for a long moment. In fact, she wasn't certain he would say anything at all. Mariah took another big swallow of her pride and said, "Thank you for listening. I wish you luck today."

She met Zach's gaze, hoping he didn't spot the disappointment she tried so hard to conceal. If he'd spotted it, that meant Edward could see it, too.

She started to turn away but stopped when she heard Edward say, "Zach came up with the idea?"

She turned back in time to hear Zach say, "I did, sir."

"Don't tell me you've become a member of her cult?" Edward asked Zach.

"No, sir." Zach shook his head. "I just think there's got to be a way we can come together. And in exchange for your cooperation, Mariah has agreed to stop her protests."

What?

She shot Zach a look of dismay.

"She has?" Edward asked, almost as if he knew Zach was lying.

"You have, haven't you, Mariah?" Zach asked. "At least while we explore the idea of a mutually beneficial welfare league. And with racing season now officially open, I knew the idea would appeal to you."

She swallowed. Hard. When she faced Edward again, she hoped her smile seemed genuine. "No protests."

Edward eyed the two of them, and despite her ire at Zach, Mariah admitted Edward seemed a lot less hostile.

"Would you be working with Mariah on this idea? Or do you expect all of us to do so?"

"I'll work with her, sir."

Edward pursed his lips and looked out at the track, and when he turned back to them, Mariah almost released a crow of delight.

"Very well. I'll expect an update at the next board meeting. I'll put it on the agenda as new business."

She would have leaned down and hugged the man if the women at the table weren't still glaring. She didn't care. This time she knew her smile was genuine.

"Thank you, Mr. Golden. Thank you *so* much."

Zach was smiling, too. "Thanks, Edward. See you next month."

A hand at the small of her back guided her away. He steered her outside the double doors, and Mariah was struck by an urge to jump into his arms. She'd done it. She was on next month's agenda.

"The race is about to start," he said, pushing the elevator button. "And I know how much you want to avoid watching it."

"I do."

He turned back to the elevator car, keeping his distance, and for some reason that upset her.

"Zach, I can't thank you enough for meeting Mr. Golden with me."

"No problem."

The noise had diminished considerably outside of the room. She waited for him to face her.

"I know you've gone out on a limb for me."

She heard him inhale sharply before saying, "I have." He glanced down at her.

"I recognize that, and I appreciate that you're helping me."

She liked him. There was no sense in denying it. He might race horses for a living. He might be a contributor to the problem, albeit on a smaller scale than someone like Edward Golden. But at least he was open-minded enough to help and to accept her help.

"Thank you," she said, grabbing his hand and squeezing it again. "Thank you so much for everything."

She meant to rise on tiptoe to kiss his cheek again—even though she told herself not to do it—but just as she perched up on her toes, Zach glanced toward the elevator that had suddenly arrived so that instead of lips meeting cheek, lips met lips—or near enough.

They both froze.

She should have pulled back. She should have, but she didn't and neither did he. Instead it was as if they'd been afflicted by a temporary paralysis. She inhaled. He exhaled. She caught the scent of him again, then the warm breath of him, the intimate feel of his body next to her own. She told herself to move, but then his lips began to gently explore, pressing, searching, giving her every opportunity to pull away, but she didn't. Instead she closed her eyes and simply gave herself to the sensations bouncing through her even as a part of her screamed, *You should not be kissing this man!*

He tilted his head and she felt his razor stubble brush her chin. Almost she groaned. Almost she opened her mouth. Almost she surrendered to him.

Instead, he surrendered to her; his mouth opened beneath her own.

His essence flooded her mouth. She moaned. She couldn't stop herself, because he tasted every bit as delicious as she'd imagined and she wanted him to keep on kissing her. Heaven help her, in that instant she admitted she'd wanted him since the moment she'd spotted him standing by a horse, all hunky male with his wide shoulders and five o'clock shadow and so damn good-looking she'd stumbled in surprise.

The elevator door began to close.

He jerked back to press the button. The doors slid open once more.

Dark blue eyes peered into her own. "I have to go."

"I know."

"I'm sorry."

Sorry about what? For kissing her? Touching her? Leaving her still wanting more?

She was so frazzled she didn't even know he'd guided her into the elevator car. When he released her, she realized where she was as she all but stumbled back.

And then he was gone. The doors closed and Mariah sank against the rail of the elevator car.

"Oh, crap."

Chapter Ten

His horse finished second, and despite telling herself she didn't care, she was happy for him. How messed up was that? She hated racing.

So what the heck are you doing kissing a racehorse owner?

Falling under the spell of a good-looking man with a kind heart, she admitted, and it wasn't good. Not at all.

She'd have avoided him if she could have, but after studying Dasher's chart, she determined he was ready for therapy. Her promise to help Dasher, combined with the fact that she'd vowed to do what she could for Dandy, meant putting on her big-girl panties and facing Zach again.

So less than three days later she found herself turning into the Triple J Ranch. She eyed the whitewashed fences, the irrigated pasture and the barn and sighed. What she wouldn't give to practice medicine out of such a place.

Her thoughts helped to distract her, but only until the moment she shut off her car. The peacefulness of the place should have soothed her, too. Somewhere in the distance a rooster crowed. Near her car a bird sang a complicated mix of notes. She listened to warbles while she took deep breaths. He'd told her to meet him at five and it was a few minutes before that, so she had time to get it together.

Okay, she told herself sternly. *You like the guy and he races horses for a living. So you either, A, get over his vocation or, B, make sure you don't kiss him again.*

She pulled on the door handle. Option B it was, then.

She heard him before she saw him. The rhythmic *shhh-shhh-shhh* of a broom being swept across the aisle alerted her to his presence. He didn't see her, so she had a moment to observe him in his work clothes—the red short-sleeved polo shirt that emphasized the width of his biceps, well-worn jeans and a red baseball cap today. All she could see of his face was his chin, the ever-present razor stubble hugging the curve of his jaw.

She flushed. It was as if a beam of white-hot light suddenly bathed her. She remembered what that stubble had felt like against her face. She recalled the taste of him. Their bodies had touched and just the memory of it made her tingle all over again.

Plan B, huh?

"Good morning," she called in as casual a voice as she could, but the damn words came out a near gurgle.

His head lifted, his dark blue eyes appearing paler with the sunlight coming from behind her. He nodded, but he didn't smile. "You made it."

She'd texted him. Too chicken to call. She'd added her congratulations on his horse placing at the meet, too. He hadn't commented back.

"I did." She moved farther into the barn.

"What horse do you want to work with first?"

"Dasher."

"No problem." He moved to the front of a stall, rested his broom there. "I turned him out in pasture today, as instructed. You said you wanted to see the filly, too, yes?"

She'd reviewed all his horses' charts, and by far the filly he called Summer had her most perplexed. No reason at all why she'd be lame. "I do."

He waited for her to catch up, and the closer she got to him, the more tense she became. Ridiculous, really. There was no reason to be scared of him, yet that was exactly how she felt. Scared and, yes, damn it, aware. Aware of the scent of him. Aware of the size of him. Aware of what that mouth of his could do to her.

"Thanks for coming over today."

As if she were a string pulled in two different directions, she felt her whole body snap. What did he mean by that? "Were you worried I wouldn't?"

He walked a few steps. "After what happened Friday, I wasn't sure."

The kiss.

Leave it to Zach to grab the bull by the horns.

"Yeah, about what happened in front of the Turf Club." She drew her shoulders back, determined not to shy away from the question. "I didn't mean to do that, you know. Well, I did. I meant to kiss you. Just not where I kissed you."

"I know."

Of course he knew. She'd just wanted to spell it out. "I hope you didn't get the wrong impression."

They emerged from the barn, and though she'd been inside for just a moment, she squinted against the sudden brightness.

"I didn't think anything of it."

She looked up at him sharply.

"I knew you were just testing the waters. So was I. No big deal."

No big deal?

"Any thoughts on what might be wrong with Summer?"

That was it? No more discussion? No "I thought the kiss was nice and I'd like to do it again"?

"I actually have no idea," she admitted, completely confused about the whirlpool of emotion swirling inside her. "I couldn't see anything on her X-rays or her ultrasound. I thought I'd see how she was today."

"Lame. Way more than the other day."

So he isn't interested. You should be happy about that.

"That's actually good news." *Get your head on straight.* "I mean, it's bad news that she's hurting but good that she's extra sensitive today. I should run back and get my hoof testers. According to her chart, she tested positive before with those. Let's see if the pain is still in her toes or if it's migrated."

"Sure," he said. "I'll pull her out of pasture."

"Perfect."

She turned away and hurried back to her car, the whole way recounting all the reasons why she should be grateful he'd dismissed their kiss but unaccountably out of sorts just the same.

She was back in moments, the stunning filly he'd led from pasture standing quietly on the racetrack where she'd ridden Dandy the other day, the filly's front foot held off the ground, the toe resting atop the sandy soil, but just the toe. She couldn't put any weight on it.

Because he'd raced her too young. No, not raced. He'd begun her training too young. Mariah should have been incensed that he'd damaged such a beautiful animal, yet all she felt was an urgent need to help, not just because the animal was in pain but also because she wanted to aid the enemy. Zach. The man who'd put the filly in this position in the first place.

What was wrong with her?

"How long was she in training?"

"Two weeks."

Two weeks? That was it?

"We thought stone bruise at first," he said, "but clearly that's not it. It comes and goes."

She'd read that in her notes and seen that firsthand because she was far more lame today than the other day, just as he'd said. Very strange. "All right, let me see her move."

The filly didn't want to step forward. Mariah didn't blame her. Clearly, whatever was bothering her hurt her a great deal. So much so that Mariah almost immediately asked Zach to stop.

"When was the last time she had her feet trimmed?" she asked.

"A few weeks ago."

So that wasn't it. Some horses got sore when they had their hooves cut back, but Summer's hooves should have hardened up by now.

"Let's see what happens when I poke around."

She went up to the mare, slowly introducing the hoof testers, which resembled old-fashioned ice picks, the kind that were used to pick up blocks of ice. The filly hardly spared them a glance.

"She seems kind," she said, walking up to the filly's side and gently running her hand down the leg.

"She's the product of three generations of meticulous breeding."

"I can see that."

She'd noticed the other day that she had nice feet, wide, and not in the least chalky, which could often lead to hoof problems. Mariah slowly put the hoof testers in place, the angle of the prongs allowing her to squeeze the outside wall of the hoof and the bottom of the foot at the same time. She got no reaction at the heel, but the toe—

"Whoa," Zach cried when the filly just about jumped off the ground.

"That's a positive." Mariah had straightened and jumped out of the way just in time. "Again. No need to poke around anymore. Instead I'd like to have another look at those X-rays. Do you still have a copy in your office? Or should I get mine out of the car?"

"No, I still have mine."

"Go ahead and put her away, then. I need to pull the machine I brought over to use on Dasher's leg out of my trunk anyway."

Zach barely glanced at her. He didn't comment, either. The man had eyes only for his injured horse, the worry and concern on his face evident. A week ago she would have claimed that worry had to do with dollar signs. She knew better now. The man was a horse person. He loved animals. She could see that in his every touch.

When he came back into the barn, he tried to hide his concerns, even going so far as to point at the machine she'd brought over and say, "Is that for me?" He managed to smile. "Some kind of device to torture me with?"

"No. It's a Cool Jet." She smiled back.

You could really like him.

The thought came completely out of nowhere. *Wham.* Suddenly it was there, and once it had lodged itself in her brain, there was no sense in denying it. Had he been any other man, had he done anything else for a living, she would have been completely smitten with him.

"So does that mean you'll kill me with a jet of water?"

He was joking, and she appreciated his attempt at humor because for some reason she couldn't look him in the eyes. "I think I've lost the urge to kill you."

She finally looked up.

"Good to know." He smiled.

It was one of those moments when everything seemed to grow quiet and the distance between them seemed to shrink and all she could think about was that kiss, that darn kiss.

"The machine uses pressure and cold water to reduce swelling. Very cutting-edge. Very useful." She stared down at the machine, at anything but him. "It uses a gel-filled hock boot. You just strap it on like a blood-pressure cuff. Completely painless and easy to use."

"Sounds good."

"I'll want to do this for a week."

"No problem."

She couldn't breathe.

"We'll start today. Later. After I look at Summer's X-rays."

"Later," he echoed softly, almost under his breath.

"Lead the way," she prompted.

Please let them do something, anything, other than stare at each other. But when he turned away, her gaze immediately dropped, and she noticed how good he looked in his red shirt and jeans.

Darn it.

He led her across the parking lot. Up ahead the single-story building that served as his office loomed. It appeared as if it might have been a farmhand's residence at one time. The thought was confirmed when they climbed a few steps up to a small porch, and Zach opened a door and revealed a small front room. The place was split in two by a wall. The back half, the office, had desks and other office equipment that she glimpsed through the open door. The front part, the reception area, was clearly a place to entertain guests, complete with a round table and enough photos of racehorses on the wall to give her nightmares for months.

"The spoils of war," he said, following her gaze, but he smiled. He disappeared into the office, then returned with the pdf copies of the scans.

"I feel like I've stepped into the devil's lair."

She was only half joking, but she softened the words with an answering smile. He handed her the images.

"Let's see what we've got here."

She flipped through the pages until she found what she was looking for, a black-and-white scan with the name Summer written in a box on the bottom left, Zach's last name right below that.

"It doesn't appear abnormal," she mused out loud. She cocked her head to the side, studying the picture from all angles. "Like I said before, the only thing I can see, and I really don't think this is the problem, are some narrow margins between the bones." She spun the image in his direction. "Look." She pointed. "See the line of the coffin bone. And then look at the navicular bone. There's usually a wider margin here, but that doesn't mean anything. Not really. It's just the only thing I see."

She could see the disappointment in his eyes and it upset her in a way she wouldn't have expected. Clearly, he'd gotten his hopes up.

"I'm so sorry, Zach."

He played with the edge of the paper. "It's not your fault."

"I know."

"I just wish I knew what was wrong with her."

"Me, too."

"You think maybe it's a growth issue?"

She pursed her lips. "I would if the pain wasn't localized to her foot. She's done growing down there, or she should be." She frowned. "I just don't know."

"Damn."

The word had been bouncing around in her own head. "Have you thought about taking her up to UC Davis for a better scan?"

"It was suggested to me, but I just don't have the money." He got up from his chair, lifted his hat and ran his hands through his hair in a way that conveyed how deeply troubled he was.

"You spend years, decades, perfecting a bloodline. All that work. Finding the perfect stallion. Breeding the mare. Hoping for a live foal. And then you get what you hope for and everything looks great, only to have this happen—and we don't even know what *this* is."

The sadness on his face tugged at her heart, as did the way he traced the outline of his horse's name on the radiograph as if trying to rewrite history and his filly's past. She had to look away for a moment, but this time for a whole different reason. This was his life and, in the filly's case, his future. If it turned out she had some type of genetic defect, she would be useless to him. A week ago Mariah would have said he didn't care. A week ago she hadn't known him.

"I think it might be worthwhile to try some injections

on her. It's easy to do, costs relatively little money, and if it helps..."

He looked up, frowned. "I suppose it's worth a try. Anything's better than watching her limp around."

She reached out and grabbed his hand, a part of her wondering why she always did that. Why did she feel this need to touch him?

"She means a lot to you, doesn't she?"

"I would never send her to a slaughter, not even if she has some kind of genetic defect."

"I know that."

"Do you?"

Something resembling a lump formed in her throat. "I do."

He squeezed her hand. She squeezed back. The urge to lean forward and kiss him, a wholly out-of-place urge, had her pulling her hand free.

"You should come to a CEASE meeting."

Whoa. What?

His mind appeared to be screaming the same word based on the way his eyes widened.

"You've let me into your world, Zach." She lifted her head because she knew it was the right thing to do. "I think maybe you should take a peek into my world."

He drew back, too, as his surprise faded. "Aren't you worried?"

She appreciated his attempt at humor, but it didn't stop her heart from running away with her like a startled horse.

What are you doing?

"They'll behave, and it will be good for them to see things from the other side, too."

"Like you have?"

She shrugged. "You're not half bad."

"Thanks. You're not so bad yourself."

The memory of their kiss flashed through her mind. Worse, he was thinking about it, too. She could tell by the way his gaze lowered to her lips and the way the air suddenly felt as charged as during a storm.

"Think about it," she said, standing abruptly.

Why, oh why, didn't he get up, too? Why did she wish he would?

"I should start working on Dasher." She pointed over her shoulder.

"I'll be out in a minute."

She nodded and refused to look at him as she left his office.

What are you doing?

Befriending a racehorse owner.

You want to be more than his friend.

And the problem was, she knew it was true.

Chapter Eleven

The next CEASE meeting was a week away—too soon in Mariah's book—but at least she'd stopped thinking about that stupid kiss. By Wednesday she'd worked on Dasher enough times to see a noticeable improvement. She'd ridden Dandy, too, enough times to warrant a call to Natalie Goodman, her hunter/jumper friend, who'd agreed to see him that weekend. Alas, she was still stumped by Summer. All in all, however, by the following Friday she was feeling more in control of her crazy thoughts, even if she did catch herself staring at him from time to time.

"You driving me?" Zach asked as he pulled one of two specialized splint boots off Dasher that protected his back legs. Zach straightened, peering at her over the back of his horse.

"I… Well, I…" She bent down and released the boots on the other side. The Velcro came free with a rip. "I suppose. If you need me to."

When she straightened, he was nodding at her. "We're going to the same place. Why take two separate cars?"

Because…because... *Think, Mariah, think.*

"I was going to run some errands afterward."

"Great. I'll run them with you."

She wasn't going to run any errands; she just didn't

want to be alone with him. She'd been doing well keeping their kiss off her mind, but being alone with him in a tiny confined space…

"Um, sure, if you want, but it means I'll have to drive you back."

"Is that a problem?"

"No. Not really." What else could she say? Bad idea? It was that. Every time she caught a whiff of him, she remembered what had happened at the Turf Club. As long as she didn't smell him, she was fine. Working in a barn aisle she'd been able to do that, but not in a car.

"That'd be great."

All week long it had been like this. She'd just get comfortable with him and then he'd do or say something that would remind her of what it was like to touch him. Sometimes he'd accidentally brush by her. Sometimes she'd catch him staring at her lips. Sometimes she would swear he was remembering, too, but being the gentleman that he was, he wouldn't call her attention to the matter. It drove her crazy.

"Will you need to change?" she asked.

He wore his usual uniform, red shirt and blue jeans, but she would bet he smelled like sweat and the usual sawdust and sage.

"Nope. I'm fine." He came around to her side of the horse. "You think the exercise is working?"

It took her a moment to follow his line of questioning—that was how discombobulated her mind was. She took a deep breath, focused on the horse.

"I do. I think the Cool Jet is working for Dandy, too."

Since she'd had the machine on-site, she'd figured why not put it to good use, so she'd been treating the horse after every workout. She wouldn't tonight, because there was no time, but just in case, she squatted and stroked Dandy's leg. No heat, and after a forty-five minute workout, that was good.

"He looks great."

"He does. In fact, I invited my friend Natalie to come over tomorrow and have a look." She straightened again, patted Dasher on the flank. "I think she's excited about seeing him."

"You think?"

His eyes caught on her lips. She realized she was nibbling them. "I do."

Stop. You don't want this attention.

"Okay. I think we're done for the day. You can put him away."

She busied herself with stashing her machine in the tack room. The thing was on a loan to her from a friend and she lived in fear of it getting damaged; it was worth a small fortune.

"Ready?" he asked, pausing in the doorway.

"Yup."

It made her self-conscious to have him follow behind her. Thankfully, she'd parked near the entrance—next to his golf cart. It was midafternoon and cloudy outside, but Mariah's cheeks were as hot as barbecue coals. She fiddled with her keys, admitting she was nervous.

She was hesitant to introduce him to her friends. But it was more than that. A week of trying to pretend as if nothing had happened had taught her the exact opposite was true. Something had happened, not just when he'd kissed her but there in his office. It was as if two puzzle pieces had joined together. She might pretend otherwise, but she couldn't deny it. Not now. Not when the very thought of being alone with him had her terrified.

"Are you sure you don't want to take two cars?"

She'd blurted the words before she could stop herself and she could swear his eyes glittered.

"Only if you don't want to carpool."

What good reason could she give him for that? No matter how hard she thought on it, she could come up with nothing. "No, no. Just asking."

She slipped into the car before she could say or do something else that would make her feel like the gawky science geek she'd always been, the one who'd been mortified to find herself paired up with the captain of the football team. Damn it. She'd thought she'd left those days far behind.

He'd climbed in the car far too quickly. She had barely enough time to clean off the front seat and then paste a smile on her face. Too bad it felt more like a ghastly Halloween mask.

"Sorry about the mess."

He didn't seem to notice.

Only when she started the car did she admit that might have been a mistake, but the last thing she'd wanted was someone trying to talk her out of it. She just hoped her friends gave him a warmer reception than his board member buddies had given her.

They drove down his long driveway in silence.

"I guess they can't exactly kick me out, can they?" he said finally. "Not when you're the president."

No. They wouldn't kick him out. Her friends might kick *her* out, however. Jillian would never let her live this down, never.

It was a short drive into Via Del Caballo. Zach's ranch was on the outskirts of town, about fifteen minutes away from the town center, but as they drew closer to civilization, they didn't leave the country behind. Animals were everywhere. The city founders had kept it that way on purpose. Every road doubled as a bridal path, a wide swath of the shoulder dedicated to equestrians. One could feasibly ride from Zach's ranch all the way to City Hall, a three-story red brick building in the middle of town. There were even restaurants off the main drag that had hitching posts out front, along with feed stores and little boutiques. On the weekend it wasn't uncommon to see a family of horses tethered to poles.

"Where are these meetings held, by the way?"

Hadn't she told him? She could have sworn she had, back when she'd assumed he'd be driving himself.

"We're going to my friend Jillian's home."

"The animal communicator?"

"The one and only."

When she glanced at him, his blue eyes had gone wide. "Wow. Not sure if I like that idea."

"Why not?"

"What if my horses rat me out like that guy you were talking about at the races?"

A smile slipped past her line of defense before she could stop it. "You have something to hide?"

She was starting to relax, but that was always the way it was with him. She'd forget for a moment that she was wildly attracted to him, and then he'd say or do or look at her in a way that brought it all back.

Jillian lived on the other side of town. They had to drive down Main Street, past the courthouse and past the brightly decorated storefronts that always beckoned Mariah to browse. She never did. The boutiques along the main drag catered to the wealthy landowners in the area.

She found herself in front of Jillian's house, the single-story bungalow that always reminded Mariah of the Mediterranean with its red tile roof and beige stucco, far too quickly. She took a deep breath, noting the number of cars parked on the street. Large meeting. Well, that wasn't surprising given the exuberant email she'd sent out after her outing to the Turf Club touting her success and putting out the call for volunteers to help her head up the animal-welfare league. Crap.

"This it?" Zach asked.

She glanced at him and said, "This is it," before pulling on the driver's door.

The fresh air felt good against her face. The sun was fading fast, especially behind the bank of clouds, a chill in the air causing her to shiver. She heard laughter erupt from inside, and Mariah wondered if they'd seen her emerge with Zach, although she doubted they'd find anything funny about that.

Her cowboy boots were suddenly made of lead, she was certain of it. Why else did her feet feel as if they weighed twenty pounds?

The door opened before she could knock, Jillian crying, "Mariah!" with a smile. Her gaze found Zach, and she drew up in surprise, her eyes darting over his face before narrowing. "And let me guess—Zach."

"The one and only." He splayed his hands, his square jaw more pronounced as he smiled.

She heard Jillian "Mmm-hmm" in a singsong voice that smacked of disapproval.

Mariah ignored her as she stepped inside. Ten pairs of eyes turned in their direction. The faces ranged in age from early teens to late fifties, all of them slightly scandalized to note a male in their midst. Point of fact, the equine-rescue world seemed to be comprised of women. Maybe that was why she was so drawn to Zach. The brave, rare male willing to keep an open mind and meet her halfway.

"Hey, everyone." She tried to cover her consternation with an energetic wave.

Vicky, the youngest of the bunch at fifteen and Jillian's horse-crazy neighbor, smiled. When she met Mariah's gaze, she wiggled her brows as if to say, *He's cute.*

"This is Zach." Mariah motioned with her hands. "He's the owner of the Triple J Quarter Horse Stables I told you about."

It was as if a wind blew through the room. What had been mild curiosity quickly scattered away, turning into surprise and, in some cases, outright hostility. One of the members, an older woman with gray hair and blue eyes, went so far as to cross her arms in front of her. That was Kathy, and she despised anyone connected to the racing industry, including Zach, it would seem.

"Zach—" she turned to her guest "—these are my fellow CEASE members."

"Ladies." He smiled. "Good to meet you."

"What's *he* doing here?" Kathy said. She wore half glasses and she wasn't afraid to peer at him over the top of them like a tax accountant chastising a cheating client.

"I thought it'd be a good idea for him to meet you guys."

Mariah noticed an open seat on the opposite side of the room, next to the fireplace and a fake potted palm that she always had to battle with. "He's been very receptive to my suggestions about his horses over the past couple of weeks, not at all combative, and I thought, I don't know, maybe it'd do us all some good to hear from someone in the enemy camp."

Now that she thought about it, she hadn't really come up with a game plan. Too distracted by Zach this week. Lord, she was losing it.

"What's the saying? Keep your friends close and your enemies closer?" She tried not to wince at the skepticism she saw in her friends' faces.

There was only one chair left, by the front door. She motioned for Zach to take it, but he in turn motioned toward Jillian, who Mariah noticed was still standing.

"No, no," her friend said. "Guests first."

She, too, crossed her arms in front of her. She looked to be both entertained and concerned.

"Thanks." Zach slipped into the chair, one of four wooden ones that Jillian had snagged from her kitchen near the back of the house. He leaned forward, resting his arms on his legs, and for some strange reason the light coming in through the window to his right accentuated his five-o'clock shadow and made his square jaw look even more masculine. It also highlighted his dark, dark blue eyes. She couldn't be the only woman in the room to think, *My, my, my.*

"Let me just start off by saying I know most of you have a very low opinion of guys like myself."

Mariah told herself to relax. The man could charm the gun off a Secret Service agent, especially when his grin was so sheepishly apologetic. Mariah found herself looking around the room to see how it affected the ladies. Two of her friends smiled back. Vicky was already a goner, but she was young and had no armor against his tanned and handsome face.

"Mariah and I haven't exactly seen eye to eye in the

past, but I hope that's changing. She wanted me to come here tonight so I could learn more about CEASE. I have to admit, I didn't think you guys would let me in here. I fully expected someone to pull out a gun and point it at my head."

"Tempting," Kathy said.

Zach didn't seem to be offended. "So tell me," he said, smiling in Kathy's direction, "what is it you guys do?" He glanced in Mariah's direction. "I think Mariah has learned what it is that I do and that I'm not an evil ogre. At least, I hope that's what she's learned."

When he glanced in her direction again, she could tell he meant the words.

"I have," she quickly reassured him. "Zach has been great, and he really cares about his horses."

Jillian snorted. Mariah shot her a glare.

"Let's be nice to him," she told her friends.

"I'll be nice if he stops racing horses," Kathy said.

Zach's gaze found Kathy, his eyes instantly apologetic. "I can't do that."

"Mmm-hmm," hummed Kathy, sounding anything but understanding. She tipped her chin up and flicked her long gray braid over a shoulder. "That's what I thought."

His "let's be friends" smile slipped a bit. "Look." He peered around the room. "I know you think I'm a horrible person, but I'm really not. As I explained to Mariah when we first met, I don't send my retired racehorses to a local auction—"

"Retired?" Kathy interjected. "Don't you mean broke down?"

Zach leaned back in his chair. "No." He met Kathy's stare head-on. "I actually do retire them. If a horse doesn't have the speed I need, I don't race them. I call a buddy of mine who will work with them for a week or two and then we send them to a reputable auction that specializes in reselling racehorses."

He did? She hadn't known that.

"Oh, please." Janice, who was seated next to Kathy, was the second-most-outspoken person in the group. "As if the meat buyers never attend auctions."

"They don't attend *this* auction. It's up north, and the price the horses sell for are far too rich for the meat man's blood. They avoid this auction like the plague."

"So you think," Kathy said.

"Go ahead and look it up. They post the sale prices online."

"And how many horses do you have to 'retire' each year?" Janice asked sarcastically.

"I only breed a few horses a year."

"That's three more than necessary." This time it was Patty who spoke, her hair as dark as her eyes. "That's the problem. You breed four. Someone else breeds five. One of your competitors breeds ten and before you know it, there's hundreds of unwanted racehorses out there that aren't fast enough to race and don't have the right mentality to be ridden for pleasure because all you want them to do is go, go, go. So what happens then? You dump them."

Mariah felt her stomach sink. Patty was right. Why did she have such a hard time remembering that?

"No, I don't—"

"An auction is dumping them," Kathy snapped.

"Call it what you will," Janice added. "You're being irresponsible."

"How do you know your horses are going to good homes?" Patty asked. "Do you follow the trailer home?"

There were nods all around the room and for the first

time Mariah felt bad. She'd known her friends might give her a hard time, but she hadn't expected them to attack him.

"Look." She shot up from her chair. "We all know there are problems. We know things need to change. That's why I wanted Zach here, so he could give us his side of the story. And at least he showed up to talk to us, unlike the other racehorse owners we've invited in the past."

She held each gaze in the room. Vicky, the teenager, was the only one who smiled encouragingly.

"So instead of putting him on the spot, let's pick his brain. See what he can come up with as far as a solution. I don't know about you, but I'm excited. He could be our secret weapon. Our one chance to actually be heard. Don't you guys feel like me? Aren't you tired of being thought of as the crazy horse-hugging CEASE person."

They had the good grace to appear chagrined. Kathy looked away for a moment. One by one they softened their expressions. It was Vicky who truly broke the ice, jumping up from her chair and holding out her hand.

"Nice to meet you, Zach. I'm Vicky."

Everyone else followed suit, some of them, like Kathy and Janice, more reluctantly than others, but they welcomed Zach, too. When they finished, she met Zach's gaze. He smiled and mouthed the words *Thank you.*

You're welcome, she silently told him back.

And she knew. She just knew—she didn't just like Zach. She liked him *a lot.*

And it scared her to death.

Chapter Twelve

She was quiet.

Zach told himself that was because it was dark outside and she had to concentrate on the road.

The meeting had lasted another two hours after Mariah's "be kind to Zach" speech, the memory of which made Zach smile. She'd been ferocious in her defense of him, almost as fierce as she'd been defending the horses to the board of directors, and it made him feel kind of warm and fuzzy inside.

"I'll want my own CEASE T-shirt," he teased.

She glanced at him sharply. The light from his porch shone inside the cab, highlighting her ringlets and setting them aglow.

"Just kidding."

She smirked, and he smiled. He'd loved watching her talk to her group, had enjoyed the way her face had lit up when they'd talked about writing a mission statement, something they could present to the Golden Downs board of directors. He'd given his opinion when he could. Gradually, the group had lightened up and Zach could tell Mariah had been relieved. So had he. He'd been worried for a moment that her friends might disown her.

When they pulled up in front of his home, she turned

to him and said, "Thanks for coming." She wouldn't look at him. She stared straight ahead, hands clutching the wheel, face tense.

"You want to come in for a sec?"

"No."

"Sure?"

"Yup."

He wanted to kiss her. He'd been wanting to kiss her since that night at the Turf Club.

"I'm really not a bad person."

She turned to him quickly. "I know that."

"I don't know if we, I mean your friends and I, could ever see eye to eye, but I hope so. I am first and foremost a horse person."

He saw her lips part. She looked away, then back at him again, as if weighing within herself the words she wanted to say. "I know."

"Have a good night." He popped the door open.

She caught his hand before he could move. He looked over at her, startled.

"Your horses are lucky to have you as an owner."

It was a compliment of the highest order and it warmed him through and through, so much so that he did what he'd been dying to do. He leaned across the seat, placed a hand behind her head and pulled her toward him.

"Zach—"

And he kissed her. Hard.

She tried to draw away, placed a hand against his chest, but only for a moment, a nanosecond, really, because it zapped to life, the connection, the current of electricity that ran between them, and it damn near blew his socks off. When their tongues touched, the electricity came to life. She moaned. Or maybe he did. Didn't matter. It was as if he couldn't get enough of her, needed to angle his head so he could kiss her more deeply, felt his nerve endings fire to life when she sagged against him and kissed him back. The hand that'd been pressing against him softened.

Bucket seats. He hated them. A damn center console sat between them. He pulled back, cupped her head, looked into her eyes. "I want to keep on kissing you."

She blinked, the glow of her dash lights revealing her flushed face. "I know."

"But we shouldn't."

"I know."

"But I can't seem to stop myself."

"Then don't." She blinked. "Stop, I mean."

It was all the incentive he needed. This time he held nothing back. This time he let himself go, his hand finding her breast, Mariah arching into him as he caressed her. He wanted to taste her, all of her, his mouth slipping off her own and finding her jawline, then her neck. Zach managed to untuck her shirt, lift the edge and expose the lacy fabric of her bra. The damn console might cut into his midsection as he leaned over, but he didn't care as his tongue slid down her cleavage, his other hand nudging the fabric aside. His whole body ignited, the sight of her nipple turning him on, causing him to shake with pure need. He captured the tip, teasing it into a hard nub, loving the sweet taste of her.

"Zach." She arched into him.

He attacked the second nipple with the same vigor. When he'd finished teasing both of them into hard points, he drew back and enjoyed the sight of pert breasts standing at his attention, tips still glossy from his mouth. She met his gaze and he smiled.

"Let's go inside."

"No."

"Why not?"

"Because… Because." Her mouth hung open for a second. "We're all wrong for each other."

"No, we're not." He bent and then captured her right nipple again. He tasted the end of it, then moved to the other. He lifted his head and said, "This is all right."

"Zach…"

He began lowering his head, his mouth skating along the surface of her breastbone and then her abdomen, pressing against her, asking her to lean back. She did. Somehow her right leg slid beneath the steering wheel and somehow, despite the car's limited room, he found himself nipping the waistband of her jeans, his mouth traveling lower until he found it—found the heat emanating from beneath her jeans.

"Oh," she moaned.

He nuzzled her, pressed his chin into her, then his mouth, listened to her ragged breathing and knew she was close to losing it.

And then he stopped.

He caught a glimpse of her face just before he left the vehicle. He was around to the driver's side before she could get back into a sitting position. His hand found the door latch, opened it. She almost tumbled from the car. He caught her, helped her to stand, propped her up against her car.

"We're going inside."

She stared up at him. "I can't."

"Yes, you can."

"I don't know," she all but wailed back. "I think—" He saw her swallow. "I think I'm scared."

"I am, too."

Her lips parted. "You are?"

He pressed against her, his body making contact with her own. "I am. But this." He kissed her again but only for a moment. "And this." He dropped a hand between them, picking up where his mouth left off, his palm cupping her. "This reassures me that what we're doing is right."

His lips found her neck. She sagged against him. He grabbed her hand, tugged her toward his house.

And at last she followed.

WHAT ARE YOU DOING?

He led her toward his house, and Mariah told herself to stop, to protest, to do something other than meekly follow in his wake.

He must have sensed her hesitation, because the minute they were through the front door, he turned and kissed her.

It took only that.

The moment their lips connected, the overwhelming desire for him was back. The tingles, the shivers and the white-hot heat that pooled warmed her insides. It didn't matter who he was. She didn't care what he did for a living. The man could turn her on.

He moved again. She followed. They entered his room, and for a moment she snapped out of her desire-induced daze.

"Wow."

She'd stopped by the door without realizing it, simply taking it all in. Massive master bed. Vaulted ceiling. Wide windows overlooked what she could imagine was a spectacular view in the daylight.

"Like I said, my mom had good taste."

He led her toward the bed, a fluffy white comforter covering the king-size mattress. He went right to the edge, turned to face her and pulled off his shirt, just jerked the thing over his head and tossed it to the floor. He stood in front of her half naked and all she could think was, *Oh. My. Gosh.*

He was like one of those comic-book superheroes. All sculpted middle and hard parts. Beneath taut, muscular pecs were twin cords of sinew that stretched down to his naval. The traditional six-pack looked more like an eight-pack because a hard square surrounded his belly and stretched toward his groin, a sprinkling of hair covering it all. Even his *sides* were muscular and bulging.

"Come here."

She couldn't move. Funny, she wasn't afraid of being intimate with him. No. She couldn't move because he was the damnedest, sexiest thing she'd ever seen and it had rendered her speechless.

"Mariah?"

She looked away, suddenly abashed. He must have taken the gesture for shyness, because he moved toward her and gently cupped her face. His smile was full of compassion.

"I'll stop now if that's what you really want."

Now? After she'd seen him half naked? Was he crazy?

"All you have to do is say the word."

He was close enough that she could reach out and touch him…if she dared.

"Mariah."

Her palm made contact with his bare chest. She inhaled sharply.

No one has to know.

And no one would.

Her fingers slid over the ridges of his chest, found his nipple, and she blushed when she felt it turn hard. She thought she heard him hiss. The sound emboldened her. She opened her eyes, ran her thumb around his dusky center, her own body tingling in response.

He unsnapped his jeans.

She couldn't look him in the eyes.

One minute she was standing near the door, the next he'd guided her to the edge of the bed. He tugged his jeans down, revealing black boxers and the unmistakable swell of his desire. She quickly looked away. Somewhere along the way he'd kicked off his boots, she noticed. When he finished shrugging off his jeans, he grasped the edge of her shirt and suddenly she turned shy. Why hadn't she lost those five extra pounds? What if when he saw *her* naked, he changed his mind? Was she wearing granny underwear? Or her cute little bikinis?

Her hair fell around her shoulders as the shirt slipped free. The cool breeze caused her stomach to contract. Or was that because of his gaze? She didn't have time to analyze it, because his hand found her naked shoulder. He slid the straps of her bra off, first one shoulder and then the other—slowly, seductively. He stepped forward, their skin grazing as he reached around her and unsnapped her bra. His head lowered and then…

Oh, heaven.

His mouth. It grazed her neck and it did something to her. Every time he kissed her, she went up in flames. This was a man she used to watch from a distance. A drop-dead gorgeous man. Out of her league, and he was kissing her and touching her, and his body—his hard, taut upper body—was against her own, and it turned her on.

She sagged onto the bed. He followed her down and when his mouth caught her nipple, she arched into him hard. How could something so wrong feel so right? How did she get here? In bed with him? The enemy. His teeth played her and teased and she really didn't care who he was and how incompatible they were for each other, because he'd started to tug her jeans down and she wanted more than his mouth—she wanted *him*.

His mouth moved lower, as did his hands, tugging the waistband down. Bikini. She wore bikini underwear. *Oh, thank God.*

"Lift," he ordered.

She did as instructed. Her boots slid off with her pants and socks; Zach tossed everything on the floor. She had a moment then. A moment when every ounce of self-confidence faded away. She lay there, staring up at him, wondering what he saw. Did he spot the scar from her appendectomy? Did he see the cellulite on her thighs? Would he find her lacking?

"You're beautiful."

She met his gaze, wanted to melt at the softness in his eyes, and she began to fall a little in love. She touched the side of his face. He stared down at her and she fell even further.

His head began to lower and she knew this was it. No more recriminations. No more worries. No more *thinking.*

His lips were soft, his hand even softer as it skated up her side. She needed no more prompting from him. She wanted to taste him again. She wanted to absorb his essence. To become a part of him. Their tongues tangled. She tried to get closer, but the minute she moved he pulled his lips away.

"Stay still."

She didn't want to stay still. Just that one kiss had her panting, had her wiggling and moving and wishing for more, but then she felt his hand there, down there, and she gasped. Okay. This would do, too. He cupped her. Her hips jerked up. He went back to kissing her, only something changed. Gone was the softness. He kissed her hard, his tongue insistent, as was his hand. She gave herself up to it all, her legs opening. He dragged a finger up her center and she honestly didn't think she could take it. She wanted more, so much more, but the minute she moved, he stopped kissing her again.

"Still," he warned.

No. She didn't want to be still. She wanted to squirm and wiggle and jerk her hips up and bring their two centers together, but, oh, it was such sweet torture not to move. His mouth returned and so did his hand and she grew dizzy with wanting but every time she shifted, he'd stop. She quickly learned to stay still and it drove her insane. It also turned her on like nothing she'd ever felt before.

He was playing her, she realized, expertly working her into a frenzy, and she let him because she wanted what he had to give so dang much.

His fingers slid beneath the fabric of her underwear. He found her valley. Both his tongue and his finger plunged deep and a million sparks exploded behind her eyes. Her hips came off the bed of their own volition, only this time he didn't tell her to stay still. This time he let her cry out and move and glide up against his hand and she was falling, falling…

Her eyes slowly opened.

He stared down at her and smiled. "You okay?"

The waves of pleasure had ebbed, but they still rolled through her as she nodded.

"Flip over." Her eyes must have widened, because he said, "I'm going to take you now, Mariah. Once again, you're not going to move."

She was so languid with pleasure that she did exactly as told. She felt him shift. Heard him open a drawer and then the unmistakable sound of a condom being opened. That was good, she thought, and then he pulled her underwear off and she stopped thinking because she felt him there, right there, and she wanted him inside her as she'd never wanted anything in her life.

"Zach," she moaned as he entered her.

"Shh." He nipped the back of her neck. "Don't move."

She was so ready for him that when she felt him enter her completely, she almost shattered all over again. When he pulled out, she wanted to follow, knew he'd punish her if she did that and so she didn't move and it was so erotic, this mounting of her, this taking of her. She heard herself moan as he plunged. His palms covered the top of her hands. His fingers twined with her own. His mouth bit and nibbled and suckled the back of her neck and she knew she wouldn't, *couldn't* last and then he somehow turned her over and they were soaring higher and higher.

He cried out.

That was all it took, his gasp of pleasure—it sent her over the edge of oblivion. She didn't move as he pulsed inside of her. Their kisses slowed, became more gentle and somehow more intimate.

"That's two," he teased.

She opened her eyes, saw amusement in his own, felt her world begin to tilt again.

"Let's see if we can make it three."

"Not possible." The words came out as a gasp, and as it turned out, she was wrong.

Chapter Thirteen

He'd never been with a woman more perfectly matched to his needs. Anything he asked of her she willingly complied with. It stunned him. He would have bet she'd be the take-charge type in bed. Instead she gave herself to him completely.

When he awoke, he had a smile on his face, but when he rolled over, he discovered an empty bed. He sat up. Her clothes were gone, too. A sheet wrapped around his midsection nearly tripped him as he flung himself from bed. He tugged it free and headed out of his bedroom to the window opposite that overlooked his front yard.

Her car was still there. The relief that coursed through him nearly knocked him to his knees. That gave him pause for a moment, but only a second because he turned toward the master bathroom, chiding himself for not checking there first. Empty. He headed for his bedroom window next, the one that overlooked the back pasture and the track out behind the barn.

And there they were—Mariah and Dandy.

She rode as boldly as she made love, her hair wild and free. Pure poetry in motion. He watched her for a moment, and something coursed through him. Something soft and unexpected and that scared him half to death.

He frowned.

They hadn't talked about their future. He hadn't wanted to ruin the most amazing and erotic night of his life. She hadn't mentioned anything, either, but if he was honest, why would she? What future did they have? It wasn't as if they'd gone into the evening talking about marriage, kids and his house on the hill. They'd acted more like two people having an affair. Maybe that was why last night had been so carnal.

He showered and dressed, surprised to note she'd clearly done the same without him the wiser. When he finally stepped outside, he wasn't surprised to see overcast skies. This close to the coast it almost always dawned cloudy.

"Wow," he called out as he leaned against the rail. "Looks good."

She pulled Dandy up, the smile on her face as bright as a spotlight. "He has a good mind." She patted the gelding on his neck. "I can't wait for Natalie to see him today."

He wasn't sure what to expect this morning, but he was glad to see her smile. "What time is she coming?"

"Any minute now."

He couldn't help but wonder if that was the reason for her bright smile. Did her grin have more to do with the impending arrival of her friend than seeing him? He'd no sooner thought the words than he heard a car on his drive.

Damn. Good thing he'd gotten up when he had.

Natalie didn't look a thing like he'd expected. She wore the beige breeches and boots he'd expected and the white button-down shirt, but that was all that fit his mental image. She was young, far more youthful-looking than he would have thought possible given how sought after Mariah made her sound. She was pretty, too, with her bleached blond hair and bright blue eyes. That straight hair was pulled back into a ponytail that hung well past her shoulders.

"You made it," Mariah called.

Clearly, Natalie had no axe to grind, either, not with evil racehorse owners—at least not judging by the smile she gave him.

"I made it." She held out her hand when she caught his eye. "Natalie Goodman."

"Zach Johnson."

"Ooh, the evil racehorse owner in the flesh."

"Natalie!" Mariah said, her cheeks turning red. She'd done that a lot last night, too.

"Don't worry." Natalie's eyes were full of good humor. "I don't share Mariah's need to burn all racehorse owners at the stake."

He liked this woman. He liked her a lot. "Well, thank God for that."

When the trainer caught sight of the horse Mariah led, she suddenly became all businesslike, however. "Wow. He's a beauty."

Mariah nodded and turned to face the horse. "Isn't he?"

"Sure does look the part of a potential hunter."

Zach hung back as Natalie walked around the horse. "Remind me of his injury again?"

"Hairline fracture of the sesamoid. Super small. Nothing serious judging by the X-rays. Just enough to make him sore, but Zach says he's been sound for weeks."

"Which leg?"

"Right front."

Natalie squatted down, felt the leg, nodded. When she stood up, she scanned the horse from head to toe. "Nice shoulder."

"Think he'll jump?" Mariah asked.

"I do. Let me see him move first."

"You want me to ride him or trot him off?"

"Go ahead and ride."

Mariah swung up. Within seconds she trotted off and Zach had to admit, she made Dandy look good. When she cantered him a few minutes later, he began to wonder if he should ask her to show all his retired horses to potential buyers.

"I like him," Natalie said. "He moves beautifully. And he seems to be super quiet."

Mariah was all smiles. "He hasn't spooked on me once."

Natalie faced him next. "Would you mind if I took him on a trial? I have an owner looking for a prospect that Dandy might be perfect for, but I'd like to see him over some fences before I make the call. If he jumps as cute as he moves, we might have a winner here."

Zach had to fight not to shoot the woman a silly grin. "I don't mind you taking him at all."

"What kind of money were you hoping to get for him?"

Zach looked at Mariah. His retired racehorses sold at auction for $1,000, maybe a little more if they were pretty or a flashy color. Frankly, he had no idea how much the horse was worth to show people.

"I was thinking five," Mariah answered for him. "He's cute enough on the flat that he'd make someone a nice dressage horse, worst case."

Five? *Thousand?*

"Five is good. My client had ten to spend."

For a prospect?

"Perfect, then," Mariah said with a smile. "When did you want to pick him up?"

"Today if you don't mind."

He was in the wrong business, Zach thought as they made arrangements. Five thousand was more than Dandy had won. It seemed like a small fortune for an untried horse. He should have been marketing his animals to the show circuit for years.

"And that's how we keep horses from being sold at auction." Mariah's smile was self-satisfied. "He'll have a great home and a new career at Natalie's place."

"If it all works out."

She glanced back at Dandy. "It'll work out. He's a beautiful animal. Someone will buy him and love him." She met his gaze. "Just like someone will buy Dasher, too. You don't have to auction him off to an uncertain fate. You can help him find a new life. That's what I do, you see—help horses. It's who I am."

He moved in closer to her, wanting to kiss her, to say thank you and that he understood, but her eyes threw up such a roadblock, he stopped. "What's the matter?"

Her smile had faded away like fog on a fall day. "I've been thinking."

Uh-oh.

"Look, last night was…"

"Great," he finished for her. "Wonderful."

"I know. It was."

"But…" he prompted.

He saw her take a deep breath. "We're just so different."

"Yeah. So?"

"I rescue horses and you—"

"Ruin them."

"I wasn't going to say that."

"No, but you were thinking that."

She opened her mouth, and he knew she was about to deny it, but to give her credit, she didn't. Instead she shook her head and admitted, "Maybe I was," with a lift of her chin. "You have to admit, last night didn't change anything about that."

No. It didn't. She was right. They'd had a great time last evening, but it was never supposed to be more than sex. He should be relieved she wasn't talking long-term commitment and telling him he would sell his racehorses if he truly cared for her. He *should* be relieved…but he wasn't.

"Okay. All right. I respect what you're saying." Her eyes flashed with such instant relief that it got his dander up. "But if you think for one minute that we'll be able to go on like before, that you're not going to look at me and think of what it felt like to have me in—"

"Stop!"

"What it was like to have me do this." He bent and kissed her. She stepped back and all he got in was a peck, but it worked. Her cheeks flared with color. "If you think that will happen, you're wrong."

"I *have* to forget. This morning I realized I'm still me and you're still you and that we'll both never change."

She handed him Dandy's reins.

"Running away won't help."

"I'm not running away, I'm just leaving before this goes any further."

SHE NEARLY SPUN her car out, she mashed her foot on the gas pedal so hard. The thing was, she knew he had a point. She wouldn't forget. How could she forget what had easily been the most erotic, sensual, mind-blowing night of her life? How could she?

She pounded the steering wheel with one hand.

He was right about one other thing, too. No matter what stupid mistake she might have made by jumping into bed with him, she was committed to helping Dasher and any other horse of his. It wouldn't be easy having to deal with Zach on a near-daily basis, but she'd manage it somehow. She just didn't relish the thought of being alone with him at his ranch.

As it turned out, fate took matters out of her hands. The same vet clinic where she'd done the colic surgery asked if she could fill in for one of their vets going out early on maternity leave. Mariah jumped at the chance, although if she was honest with herself, she was partly relieved to have a good excuse to avoid Zach—well, somewhat. No matter what her schedule, she still needed to work with Dasher. It was critical that the animal receive care, but she didn't want to go back to his ranch. Working at the clinic gave her the perfect excuse not to do that. She texted Zach. She was too cowardly to actually call. His one-line response—tell me where to bring him and when—was a relief. It still meant she'd have to see him, but at least there'd be no chance of hanky-panky.

Since she'd already worked with most of the staff at the Via Del Caballo Veterinary Clinic, she settled in quickly. They specialized in equine lameness, although she was apt to do anything from draining an abscessed hoof to preg-checking a cow. Large animals came in all shapes and sizes, and she enjoyed the work. Hell, who was she kidding? She was just happy to work. Veterinary jobs were few and far between, something they didn't tell you in vet school, and so any pustule in a foot was a good pustule in a foot—maybe not for the owner, though.

"Um, Dr. Stewart, there's a gentleman here to see you."

She was in the process of taking the TPR—temperature, pulse and respiration—of a sick horse, but something about the way Erin said the words had her looking up. There was a gleam in the twentysomething-year-old's blue eyes. She had that ready-to-burst-at-the-seams expression on her face and a grin that was almost always hormonally generated.

Zach must be here.

"I'll be there in just a minute."

The vet tech nodded. Mariah finished with the TPR. "His respiration is up, and he has a slight temperature," she told the nervous owner, a teenager who'd arrived with her mother and who clearly loved the black-and-white paint horse. "My guess is equine influenza. It's going around. Did you take him off-property recently?"

The dark-haired girl looked stricken. She glanced at her blonde mom, who stood nearby. "I went to a team penning last week."

Yup. Just as she thought. "That'll do it." She smiled reassuringly. "Don't worry, Hailey. His lungs are good and he's in great health other than the fever and lack of appetite. He'll get over it just like any human would."

The relief on Hailey's face made Mariah's smile grow. This was the part she loved about her job. Helping animals and their owners. The teenager's mother came forward and gave her daughter a hug. Mariah recommended doing some blood work to confirm the diagnosis. She left them in the hands of a very capable vet tech who'd draw the serum.

All in all she was in a pretty great mood as she left the building where they did their exams—well, except for the nervousness she felt at having to face Zach and all the while somehow managing to contain her attraction to him. She'd arranged for Dasher to stay in one of the stalls available to convalescing horses. She'd talked to the owner of the practice about Dasher's care and rather than blow her off like so many old-school vets, Dr. Saffer had been genuinely interested in her program. He'd even had a suggestion about Summer, which Mariah had relayed to Zach, although she hadn't heard if it'd worked. She hadn't wanted to call to find out. She would put Dasher in his stall, wave goodbye to Zach and forget about him.

Or so she thought.

It'd been two days since she'd last seen him. He stood in the lobby, every assistant, vet tech and office worker having found their way to the reception area, and she could see why the moment she arrived. The dratted man wasn't in his usual uniform of a red Triple J polo and jeans. Oh, no. He wore the jeans and a cowboy hat, all right, but he'd topped it off with a white T-shirt, skin-tight, that showed off every bulging biceps, triceps and deltoid she'd kissed, stroked or simply held on to when they'd made—

Don't go there.

"You're here. Good," she said as breezily as she could. *Good God, someone give the man a robe.* "Let me show you where we're putting Dasher."

The five-o'clock shadow, the one he'd scuffed against her skin that made her tingle all over, was also in place. As were the sexy blue eyes, a wicked little smile—all directed at her.

"Don't you look all professional-like," he said.

Damn it. Why did she blush? She wore a lab coat, for goodness' sake. Her hair was in a ponytail. All she needed was a pair of spectacles and she'd be the spitting image of a stereotypical doctor.

His eyes said something different.

The man undressed her with those eyes. She could have sworn his gaze lingered on her neck for just a moment, and just the memory of him nuzzling her with his stubbled chin sent a shot of desire right through her.

Yeah, sure. Pretend like nothing happened.

"You should have seen me earlier when I had my arm up a cow's patoot."

One of the girls behind her giggled. A little too loudly, Mariah thought. Probably Erin.

"Any animal that has you as a vet is lucky."

And his eyes were so sincere she felt herself melt.

Get a grip, Mariah.

"Follow me," she said.

"I can show him where to put his horse, Dr. Stewart," Erin called out from behind her massive reception area. Really, the clinic was a showplace with its tile floors, horseshoe-shaped front desk, high ceilings, and glass-and-chrome light fixtures. "You don't have to do it."

Wait. Was that…? She took a deep breath. Possessiveness. She felt possessiveness bubbling in her breast. No way. *Deep breath.*

"That's okay. Zach here is a friend."

When she spotted the surprise and disappointment in Erin's pretty blue eyes, it caught Mariah off guard—as did the smug satisfaction that coursed through her.

She was shocked at the direction her thoughts had taken, but she was only human. Erin was gorgeous: young, pretty and clearly available if Zach were so inclined. Only he wasn't. He had eyes only for her.

"*I'll* take him to his horse's stall." Had that sounded too possessive? Probably, but she didn't care.

They emerged into bright sunshine. When she glanced back at Zach, the glare off the windows of the state-of-the-art facility nearly blinded her. It looked like a barn from the outside, only the front was all office, and the back was the exam rooms and the hospital ward, all with wide roll-up doors so horses could be led in and out. Trailer parking was out in front of the heavily landscaped driveway. She spotted his six-horse rig, a gleaming white trailer with the words Triple J Racing Stable emblazoned across the top. Dasher stared out at her from behind the bars of his trailer window.

"I'm really glad you agreed to this. With my new work schedule I wasn't certain how I'd fit Dasher's therapy into the mix. This will make things much easier."

"How have you been?"

"Fine, thanks." She went to the back of his trailer and unlatched the door. Dasher nickered, hooves thumping on the aluminum floor as he danced around in anticipation. "How's Summer?"

She looked back in time to catch his expression of frustration. "The special shoes haven't helped."

She swung the door open. The pine-laden scent of shavings filled the air, but she paused for a moment, disappointed on his behalf. She'd suggested Dr. Saffer's solution as a kind of Hail Mary, something to try before they started sticking needles in her foot.

"I guess we'll need to inject her, then."

When she glanced back, she admitted with his cowboy hat on he'd looked like one of those modeling photos she'd seen on Facebook, the ones where the man was supposed to be a cowboy but was probably a UPS driver in real life. Not Zach. He looked pure country and, damn it, she couldn't stop thinking about what it'd been like to have him kiss her. That had her rushing inside the trailer and doing something she would never have done under normal circumstances: she began to unload the horse without his permission. Dasher, injured leg wrapped, craned his neck to look around at her.

"What are you doing?" He jumped inside, too. "Let me do that."

She stepped out of his reach, but their hands still brushed and all she could do was close her eyes. She'd thought a couple days away from him would dull the memories of their night together. Honestly, she'd fervently prayed that would be the case. Clearly not. Being near him brought it all back.

"This way." She turned away before he caught a glimpse in her eyes of what she was thinking.

Dasher unloaded easily, his injury completely unnoticeable, she observed with a critical eye. Focusing on the horse was good. It helped get her mind off Zach and the wickedly disturbing memory she had of him telling her, *Don't move.*

She found herself standing in the middle of a barn aisle without remembering how she got there. Stupid. "Um, yeah, over here." They actually had to backtrack. "Sorry, I'm still learning all the stall numbers."

She didn't dare look at him in the eye as she opened the stall door. "We have security cameras everywhere, so no need to worry about anyone trying to steal him. Someone is always watching."

He turned Dasher loose. The two of them watched him for a moment before Zach turned away. He paused in front of her and suddenly Mariah's heart skittered across her ribs.

"I've missed you."

She found herself staring at the lead rope in his hands. It was red and white, the colors twisted together like a candy cane. "Zach."

"I know it's only been two days, but it's felt like longer."

Her heart had resumed beating but at a far faster pace than before and from nowhere she heard herself say, "This is crazy."

"I know."

"It can't possibly work out."

"We can at least try."

"What would we tell people?"

"Who cares? It's none of their business."

"I would care."

"Why?"

She swallowed because she honestly didn't have an answer for that.

"Look, I'm going to pick you up at six tonight, and don't tell me you're working. I already checked with the girl up front and I know you're not on call tonight and that you get off work at four."

She would have to have a talk with Erin.

"Don't get mad. I want to take you someplace completely unrelated to horses or the racing industry. We're just going to be two people, a man and a woman getting to know each other, nothing more."

She scanned his eyes with her own. It was a bad idea. Someone might see, but then his words came back to her. *Who cares?*

"You don't know where I live."

"Actually, I do. When Natalie picked up Dandy, she told me you live at her place."

She still wasn't convinced, but Zach lowered his head, peering deep into her eyes and saying, "Please. Let's just give this a try. One date. No talking about racehorses. No discussing animal welfare. No worrying about the future. I like you, Mariah. I want to get to know you better."

His whole body had gone still while he waited for her answer. She'd gone still, too. No. That wasn't exactly true. Inside, everything shifted and tumbled end over end.

I like you.

She liked him, too.

Above their heads the loudspeaker came to life. Someone requested she pick up line one.

"Six o'clock."

And then she ran to get the phone.

Chapter Fourteen

Nerves.

They attacked his stomach and made his hands shake like someone with a caffeine addiction as he drove toward Mariah's home. Zach called himself ridiculous and, when that didn't work, tried to analyze why being with Mariah made him feel things, strange things, things he'd tried so hard not to feel over the years.

She made him want to settle down.

That was crazy. Absolutely nuts because he'd told himself he would never get married, not after watching what his mom did to his dad. And yet here he was. And she was an animal-rights activist. The founder of CEASE.

Uptown Farms wasn't at all what he'd expected. Given Natalie Goodman's down-to-earth attitude, he'd expected a simple facility, something small and utilitarian. What he saw instead was a state-of-the-art facility that would have rivaled a farm in Kentucky. Irrigated pastures and white rail fences. Huge covered arena to his left. Another sand arena to his right, one with jumps in it, and straight ahead a massive barn that had to have at least twenty-four stalls, maybe even thirty, with a steeple roof and an extra-wide entrance.

Mariah lived behind the barn, but he pulled up to the parking area in front and stopped his truck next to a small car—one of those electric doohickeys that always reminded him of a giant Air Jordan. He'd been told Dandy was doing great, but he'd still like to see for himself. No matter what Mariah might think, he hated to let his horses go. They were like his kids. He watched them drop as babies, broke them to halter and, when the time came, rode them first.

"Well, well, well, if it isn't the party crasher."

He recognized the voice, but only when he spotted the short black hair and pixielike face did he put a name to it. Jillian. The animal communicator who'd given him such a hard time at the CEASE meeting.

"Doctor Dolittle," he said with a smile.

She smirked, hands on her breeches-clad hips. "You slumming it tonight?"

Clearly, she rode English, judging by her breeches and boots and dark blue rugby shirt. "I'm here to pick up Mariah." He tried to project friendliness. "We're going on a date."

She didn't bother to hide her disdain. "Great."

He almost let the comment pass…almost. "You mind me asking why you don't like me?"

She narrowed her blue eyes. "Let's just say I don't trust your motives."

It took him a moment to follow her thinking. "You believe I'm using her?"

"I think you and your racing buddies would love to bring Mariah to heel."

He almost laughed. "Have you seen what happens when you tell Mariah what to do? I doubt anybody could bring her to heel."

Jillian didn't answer. Zach decided to change the subject. "Do you know which stall my horse is in?"

She still stared. Zach wondered if she would answer, but then she jerked her chin to the left.

"Third one on the right."

She climbed into her basketball-shoe car before he could say another word.

"Well, that went well, didn't it, buddy?" he asked Dandy a few minutes later. "Think I really charmed her, huh?"

"Charmed who?"

Mariah had come up behind him without him noticing, and Zach felt oddly reluctant to face her. When he did, the strange feeling in his stomach intensified. She wore her hair down long and loose—his favorite way—a white blouse hanging partially off her shoulders. He loved that she still wore her jeans and boots. Actually, that fit in with his plan perfectly.

"Your friend Jillian."

Mariah frowned. "Yeah. She's a tough nut to crack." She glanced inside the stall. "He looks happy, doesn't he?"

Change of subject. Probably a good idea. "He does."

"Natalie took him over fences this morning. She told me he's cute. Knees-to-his-eyebrows kind of cute. She was thrilled. Pretty sure her client will be making you an offer."

"That's great." He could use the money. Every month was a struggle. If only Dasher hadn't injured himself. He'd been his best hope to secure the future of the Triple J Racing Stable. Now? Who knew?

"She said if it wasn't for his injury, you could have gotten at least ten for him."

He couldn't contain his surprise. "Wow."

"She'd like to look at all your retired racehorses from here on out, including Dasher when he's done healing up."

No more auctions. Well, at least for some of his horses. She'd done exactly as she'd promised.

What if she could do the same for the rest of his friends?

What if her plans weren't just pipe dreams?

"That's great."

She smiled, looking self-satisfied. "I'm glad it worked out."

"I really owe you." He pulled his cell phone out and glanced at the time. "Speaking of that, we should get going."

"Going to where?"

"It's a surprise."

"I hate surprises."

"You'll love this one."

She didn't look convinced, but he headed for his truck just the same. She followed, and he had to admit, he felt strangely lighthearted. Maybe it had to do with selling Dandy. Or maybe he should just admit he really looked forward to spending more time with Mariah.

"Can you at least tell me if I'm going to need a jacket or something?" she asked as he opened the door for her.

"I don't think so, but just in case, I brought an extra."

She climbed inside and he just about ran around to the driver's side. Lord. He was like a teenager who'd just gotten his driver's license.

"I can't wait for you to see what I have planned."

She stared at him, clearly pondering what he might be up to, and he wondered when the last time was that someone had done something for her. She was always busy running around. Helping horses. Talking to people. Trying to save the world. He would bet her own wants and needs came last.

"When was the last time you had a vacation?"

He had to focus on the road, but he caught her look of surprise. And then she laughed. "Vacation? What's that?"

Just as he thought. Granted, he didn't exactly take yearly sojourns to the Bahamas, either, but his vocation took him to different parts of the country from time to time. Plus, there were frequent parties at the track, not to mention social events sponsored by wealthy horse owners, many so over-the-top they would do a rock star proud. So while it was mostly work, there was also play. He suspected the same couldn't be said about Mariah. His thoughts made him all the more excited about what he had planned.

They'd lapsed into silence, a comfortable one, Zach afraid to say too much lest he give the game away. Before too long they'd left Via Del Caballo behind, but the route he took was off the beaten path, taking them through low-lying mountains and briefly onto a freeway until he turned onto the coastal highway.

"Please tell me you're not taking me to a fancy restaurant."

"Patience," he advised as a wide expanse of blue ocean stretching as far as the eye could see appeared to their left.

"Although I'm enjoying the view."

The sun wasn't down just yet, but it would be in an hour or less, and so it was low enough in the horizon that it turned the tops of waves into golden ribbons. It would be a perfect evening, he thought, slowing down when he spotted the road he was looking for.

She sat up and leaned forward when he slowed. "What is this?"

He scanned the gently curving hills, all of which were covered with grass, the road they traveled upon made of packed dirt. A barbwire fence bracketed both sides of the dirt road and helped guide the way.

"Private ranch." He saw her brow furrow in obvious confusion. "The property stretches all the way to the beach."

Her eyes widened in surprise. "Must be nice to have your own beach."

"Technically the state owns all the beaches in California, but for all intents and purposes it's my friend's."

"Which friend?"

"Just a friend."

The beach was a half mile from the highway, and Zach had to work to keep a smile off his face as they climbed a small hill. Any minute now. He couldn't wait to see the expression on her face when she saw what he had planned, and so as he crested the hill, he was looking right at her when she spotted the cattle holding pen in the center of a grass-covered valley. Tied to the wooden fence were two horses.

"Ever ride on the beach?"

"YOU'RE KIDDING," she asked, unable to keep the excitement out of her voice. Riding on the beach was on her bucket list. Ironic that she lived in California and had never done it before.

"Ocean is over the dunes." He pointed toward a small berm, one covered in sea grass, the blades blending beneath a slight wind.

"This is amazing."

Wherever the main ranch was, it wasn't in sight. To her left and right was a narrow valley that seemed to follow the coastline, the ground sandy beneath her feet, the roar of the ocean the only clue that they were near the crashing waves—that and the salt-laden air.

"Whose horses are these?" she asked as she slipped from the truck, only to shake her head. "Wait. Let me guess. Your mystery friend."

"Yup."

"A racing friend." She pointed to the freeze brand on the horse's shoulder, a white patch of hair in the shape of a sideways, or "lazy," L. "I'm guessing Wesley Landon, the only other friendly face on the board of directors."

"Clever girl."

"Are they retired racehorses?"

"Pretty sure they are, but we're not supposed to talk about anything related to racing, remember?"

She smiled, and she had to admit, she was in a far better mood than before. The past few days had been crazy, compounded by the fact that she'd spent the bulk of them trying not to think about Zach. Now here she was, and if she was being completely honest with herself, she was happy. Really, really happy. She'd never been on a date with a man who loved horses as much as she did and it was like a dream come true.

"Pick a horse. The sorrel is named Copper, and the gray is Logan."

"Okay." She took a step back, eyeing the two horses. She couldn't see all of the gray, so she moved around to the other side. They wore Western saddles, which looked kind of funny on the tall animals.

"What are you doing?"

"I'm picking the horse I think will be fastest in the race."

"Did you just say the *R* word again?"

"I did, and I choose Logan." She pointed at the gray. "He's broader through the shoulder and has a nice angle to his hip. Looks like a speed horse to me."

He appeared surprised by her assessment.

"What?" she asked.

"Nothing." He tucked away a smile.

"Just because I don't like racing doesn't mean I don't know a thing or two about horses. I am a vet, after all."

"I know."

They mounted up, and Mariah's stomach was full of butterflies for myriad reasons, some of which she refused to identify. Her horse stood patiently while she sorted her reins and stirrups. In the movies the heroine would have landed in the saddle, then immediately spurred Logan into a run, but that was only in the movies. Instead she clucked her horse forward and took a feel of the gelding's mouth and how he handled. Like a dream, she admitted, getting more excited. She tasted salt on her lips as she smiled.

"Shall we trot?" he asked.

Since the beach was on the other side of a small incline cut into the middle of a dune, she nodded, and off they went, but only for a bit. The minute they made it to the top of the dune, she pulled Logan to a stop.

"Oh, man." Her words seemed so inadequate.

In front of them stretched an expanse of coastline that took her breath away. Far down a beach dotted with driftwood and patches of seaweed she could see the curve of the coastline. Off to her right on a ridge that overlooked the ocean was a house that she could barely make out.

"Goodness. How much of the coast do they own?"

"It's just Wes and his mother, and I believe it's about five miles."

"Five miles!"

"Wes's family drilled most of the oil wells in Southern California. They also still own a portion of them all, and if you want to hear a good opposites-attract story, you should have Wes tell you about his mom and his dad—the environmentalist and the oilman."

His words and the look in his eyes made her want to turn away all of a sudden. "Sounds disastrous."

"Far from it."

Or maybe it was the way he looked sitting atop his horse. The light blue button-down complemented his eyes. He bent and stroked his horse's mane gently. It reminded her of how softly he'd touched her that night. That unforgettable night that she'd tried so very hard to forget.

"They were married for thirty years before Mr. Landon's death, thus proving that opposites can not only attract, they can find common ground, too."

She would have to be an idiot not to guess his point. She had the option of saying something flippant, but she couldn't do it.

"Come on," she said instead. "Let's go ride on the beach."

Chapter Fifteen

It was a ride she would never forget. From the crisp ocean breeze to the glorious sunset they witnessed. She worried about riding after dark, but a nearly full moon allowed them to see. She found herself galloping through the surf, the splash of the water a cool blast against her cheeks, the waves silvered by moonlight. They laughed, they chased each other, and just as she'd predicted, she beat him, and when it was all over, her cheeks actually hurt from smiling so much.

"I'd like to pitch a tent and stay out here forever," she admitted as they dismounted near his truck. In the distance the crash of the waves seemed to have grown louder in the still of the night.

"We can come back anytime."

"Really? I would hate to impose."

"Wes doesn't mind."

She straightened suddenly as she pulled the reins over her horse's head. "How many women have you brought out here?"

"What?"

She couldn't see his face very well, but she could see his raised eyebrows. He frowned.

"How many?" she repeated.

"I've *never* done this before. Wes was the one to suggest it. He's actually offered the use of his horses to me a few times over the years, but I've never done it. I've never wanted to bring someone out here, not until I met you."

Oh.

She had a hard time breathing for a moment. She busied herself tying up Logan. She'd been jealous. Horribly, awfully jealous at the thought of him sharing this experience with another woman. She almost rested her head against Logan's neck.

"Mariah, you're the only one." She thought she heard him release a huff of laughter. "Hell, I don't usually spend time with *any* woman. One or two dinners is about all I manage."

She stood there, the halter she'd been about to slip over Logan's head hanging limply in her hands. Silly how his words affected her. They'd known each other for only a few weeks. And he raced horses for a living. His words shouldn't make her feel weak at the knees.

She heard him lead his horse up next to her. "I want to spend time with you, Mariah. I've never wanted that before, and damned if it doesn't scare the crap out of me, too."

"Zach."

He gently tugged her into his arms. She didn't resist. He didn't try to kiss her, just held her, and it felt so, so…*right.*

"In fact, I was thinking earlier about Wes and his family."

She closed her eyes.

"They own a lot of land. I mean, *a lot,* and I wondered if I should ask him to open up some of his acreage to retired racehorses. You know, give them a place to live until a home could be found for them, or not. Maybe just turn them out."

Mariah couldn't speak. His words had robbed her of breath, again. She looked up at him. Even in the moonlight she could still make out his five o'clock shadow. She lifted a hand to stroke his jaw. "Zach."

"Stop looking at me like that."

"Like what?"

"Like you want me to kiss you, because you have no idea how tempted I am, and if I do, I'm not going to stop."

She wouldn't want him to stop.

"We need to put the horses away," she said.

As much as she hated to admit it, they had to take care of their animals.

Reluctantly, she let him slip out of her arms. They worked in silence, Mariah feeling as if she stood at an intersection, one where she could turn left or right and depending on which way she went, one road would profoundly change her life.

So which direction would she choose?

She worried her bottom lip. Her hands shook as she unsaddled her horse. They both finished about the same time and Mariah found herself holding her breath.

"Come here."

She knew what he wanted. He wasn't just asking for her to slip back into his arms. He asked for so much more. She shouldn't. She really shouldn't. There were so many reasons why this was a bad idea. And yet still she went to him.

The moonlight caught the glint of teeth as he smiled, but he didn't kiss her right away. "I have a blanket behind the seats. Would you like to go back to the beach for a bit?"

She didn't think she could speak, and so she nodded. He took her hand and led her to the truck, emerging with a wool blanket a moment later, and suddenly a new sensation began to fill her. Anticipation.

She knew what that blanket meant, knew what he intended to do, and she wanted that. Oh, how she wanted it, had thought of nothing but their one night together ever since she'd left his house.

They walked up the dune, sea grass bobbing in the breeze. It was cool but not cold, and even if it had been, she'd soon be warm. He would see to that.

"Here," he said, spreading the blanket out on the sand. The roar of the waves was louder here, sounding like the boom of thunder at times, the waves crashing farther out to shore than before. Tide moving out.

He held out a hand. She took it.

He didn't kiss her; instead he began to undress her. The breath of the ocean blew upon her bare skin. The peasant blouse she wore was easy to slip off. No buttons, just elastic. He tugged it over her torso in one move. She undid her own bra, her breasts springing free, and rather than making her self-conscious, it made her feel emboldened. She saw his eyes narrow, her own eyes having adjusted perfectly to the darkness. In the distance one of the horses neighed. It seemed somehow fitting, though she didn't know why.

She didn't give him the option of taking off her jeans. She kicked off her boots and socks and undid her own snap, slowly unzipping her jeans and then peeling them ever so suggestively over her hips, down her thighs and off her calves. He didn't move. She was pretty sure he didn't breathe, either, and she loved what she did to him. What started as a simmer turned into a rapid boil. She flicked her hair over one shoulder and simply stood there, loving the way his eyes skated over her body, feeling his gaze like a hot caress.

"You're beautiful."

He reached out a hand. She arched toward him, the tip of her breast coming into contact with his hand, and she groaned. He did nothing more than touch her, but it was the anticipation, the sheer excitement of knowing what he would do to her.

"Please," she moaned.

His index finger circled her tip, once, twice. She closed her eyes. It took her a moment to realize the finger had been replaced by his mouth. His hands slid down her side toward her hips, drawing her up against him. She might be naked. He might still wear his clothes, but it didn't matter. She became lost in the feel of his tongue against her breast, his teeth teasing her nipple, his mouth suckling the tip.

She began to pant. The breeze did little to cool her hot flesh. His mouth paused for a moment, then began its wondrous assault on her flesh beneath her breast. First her ribs, then her belly and then— Oh, heaven.

She clutched his head.

"I want to hear you scream my name."

He'd knelt before her and she hadn't even noticed, because he was nuzzling her and then using his hands to part her....

"Zach."

"Louder," he urged, his tongue flicking out and finding her center.

She gasped, and when his mouth found her nub, she

cried out. His hands cupped her rear, moving her, urging her higher. She heard her moans, her rhythmic cries of pleasure. They grew louder and louder until—

"Zach," she cried, clutching his head. "Zach."

Somehow she collapsed; somehow she was beneath him. She still rode waves of pleasure, the weight of him resting between her thighs.

"I want you."

She told him without words she wanted him, too, lifting her hips. He shifted. She knew he readied himself, knew that at any moment…

There.

She whimpered. She would have never thought it possible to feel the need for him again, not so quickly, but the moment she felt him, she gasped. It was there, the keening, tingling need, right there in the pit of her stomach. She wrapped herself around him.

"Look at me," he ordered.

She opened her eyes, stared into his blue depths. He shifted, one of his hands brushing the side of her face.

"Look at what you do to me, Mariah."

He moved. She wanted to close her eyes again, but something in his gaze prohibited her from doing so. He held her as he gently took her. He kissed her, but it was a brief brush of his lips, almost as if he couldn't stop himself from doing so, but he went right back to staring into her eyes as he moved inside of her. This was no frenzied coupling, she realized. This was soft and gentle and something wholly different. Something she'd never felt before.

He kissed her again, and this time he lingered and she opened her mouth, his kiss matching the gentleness of his lovemaking. Supple mouth. Tender touches. Soothing kisses. Her pleasure began to build. His, too. She could feel him edge closer, ever closer. His hand left her face, clutched her hand. His head drew back and he stared and she stared back, his name sliding past her lips.

"Zach."

It repeated in her head—*Zach, Zach, Zach*—as she climbed higher and higher until for a second time she shuddered in pure pleasure. He kissed her again and she felt something build behind her eyes, something that had to do with the beauty of it all and with how completely perfect it felt to be in his arms.

"Mariah," he said softly.

And when she came back to Earth and looked into his eyes, she knew he felt the same way.

THEY SPENT THE NIGHT at the beach. At some point Zach must have gone back to his truck and pulled out another blanket, because she woke up with a quilt over top of her. A good thing, too, because fog had rolled in during the night. She blinked the sleep out of her eyes, registering the sound of her cell phone's alarm. She sat up, having to scramble to find where her pants were, and pulled out her phone a few seconds later.

"Shit."

She had to be at work in an hour.

"What time is it?" Zach asked.

"Almost seven."

"Shit," he echoed, sitting up, too.

How had she managed to sleep through the whole night without once awakening? They had at least a half hour drive back home.

"Guess I'm wearing this to work this morning." She located her undergarments, slipping them on. "Can you drop me by?"

"Won't you need your car during the day?"

"No. I use the clinic's truck."

"Then yes."

"Great. Thanks."

She dressed in record time. She didn't bother with her boots. She'd put them on in the truck. The sand beneath her feet had turned cold and damp during the night. She ignored it, heading for the path across the dune, but as they crested the top, they were brought up short by the sight of Wes tossing hay to his horses in the corral down below.

"Good morning," he called out to them.

She glanced at the ground, hoping against hope a giant crack would open up in front of her, one she could jump into. Last night had changed things between her and Zach, but she wasn't exactly sure what that meant or if she was ready for the whole world to know about the two of them.

"Morning," Zach called back, stepping forward again.

The only reason she didn't turn and run away from the knowing look of amusement on Wes's face was that they were already late.

Instead she pasted a smile on her face as they reached the man and said, "No time to talk, Wes. Running late, but thanks for letting us use your horses last night."

He laughed and her dratted cheeks flared with color and she mentally cursed inside. By tomorrow the entire backstretch would know she and Zach were sleeping together.

"Call you later," Zach said as he unlocked his truck. Mariah all but dove into the passenger seat.

"Actually, I'll see you out at the track," Wes replied.

Zach lifted a hand and turned to Mariah. "Don't worry, I'll get you to work in time."

"What about you? Won't you be late, too?"

He glanced at her and smiled. "I'm the boss. I can be as late as I want."

True. And so what if Wes knew she was in a relationship with Zach. Sooner or later it was bound to come out. Wait. *Were* they in a relationship?

"Should I find a ride home tonight?" she asked.

He was busy navigating down the gravel road, but he took the time to smile at her again. "No. I'll pick you up."

"You sure? You don't have to."

A hand landed on her thigh. "Mariah, I *want* to see you."

In a relationship. With a racehorse owner.

You've lost your mind.

"We need to work on Dasher tonight," she reminded him.

"I'll take you to dinner after."

Her heart leaped, which was crazy because she just couldn't get around what he did for a living and her own work with CEASE. They would have to find middle ground, she told herself, something he seemed committed to doing, so what was she worried about? They *could* work it out. Some of her friends from CEASE might not like it, but they'd get over it, especially Jillian. Sooner or later her friend would see that Zach was a really nice guy.

One who strapped saddles on baby horses and then forced them to run as hard as they could before their legs had even finished growing.

Stop!

It would work out. It had to.

Chapter Sixteen

She looked a little nauseous when she hopped out of his truck and headed into work. Zach told himself that was because of the breakneck speeds he'd reached trying to get her to work on time. They'd made it but only just barely, Zach having to content himself with a quick kiss goodbye.

The rest of the day passed in a blur. One of the few horses he had in training, Cash Only Special, was in a race this weekend and he'd come up a little sore the other day. He'd almost told Mariah about it, had been tempted to let her examine the bay gelding he'd nicknamed Cash, but the last thing he wanted was a lecture on how pushing a young horse was bad. Still, he felt like a cheating husband when he spotted Doc Miller walking toward him.

"Zach," the gray-haired man said, eyeing the horse tied up outside its stall. The black polo shirt with Miller Equine printed across the left breast couldn't be comfortable. Once the coastal fog had burned off, it'd turned into a blazing-hot day. "What seems to be the problem?"

He'd tell Mariah it'd been the owner's decision to call Doc Miller, that was what he'd do.

You're going to lie to her.

He silenced the voice by sheer force of will. "He's stepping a little short on the right front. Not a lot, just enough to make me worry there might be something going on."

Doc Miller pulled up the legs of his jeans before squatting down by Cash's side. "I hear you're seeing that Mariah woman."

Wow. Word had gotten around fast. Not that he would have expected any different, especially with as many times as he'd been seen with her.

"She's just a friend."

"Guess that could be a good thing. At least you won't be a target of her craziness anymore."

Zach bit back a sarcastic retort, surprised by the burst of instant irritation. "She's actually a great gal."

"She's pretty, too. I hear she's a vet."

Word really *had* traveled fast. "She is."

"Surprised you didn't call her." Doc Miller felt down first one leg, then the other.

"She doesn't like coming to the track."

Not exactly true, but he didn't feel like explaining the complexities of his relationship with Mariah to Miller.

"Except when she's protesting." Doc Miller glanced up, smiled. "I don't feel any heat. Why don't you trot him out so I can see what you mean?"

Happy for the change of subject, Zach did as asked, pointing out to Doc Miller how Cash seemed to flinch when turning left or right. "Stone bruise, you think?"

"Could be," the doctor answered. "You know, I heard some of the trainers talking. A few of them aren't too happy about having her around."

"What do you mean?"

"Coming to the track. They think she's just using you.

They think she's trying to get videos of horses being abused or something."

"You're kidding."

Doc Miller squatted again, this time feeling for a digital pulse. They thought Mariah was *spying* on them?

"Tell them she hasn't even asked to come to the track. She avoids this place like the plague."

Doc Miller nodded, felt around some more. "Good to know." He stood again. "Could be a sprain. Let's trot him around a bit again."

They thought she was a spy? Obviously, they didn't know her that well.

Throughout the rest of the appointment, Zach kept turning the doctor's words over in his mind. He didn't care what his fellow trainers thought, but he *did* worry about Mariah and her feelings. She would be hurt if she caught wind of what was being said.

Idiots.

"Definitely a foot problem."

The words brought Zach back to the present.

"Outer wall." Doc Miller pulled a hoof pick from his back pocket, poking around a bit before straightening again. "Pretty sure it's just a bruise. Should feel better tomorrow or the next day."

"He's supposed to race this weekend."

"He should be good enough for that. It's legal to give bute, so I'd do that and then let him run."

Mariah would have shot herself in the big toe before ever saying something like that. To be honest, he didn't exactly like the idea of letting an animal that was hurt run, either.

Doc Miller pulled out a paper tablet. "If it's an abscess, you'll know soon enough. I'm just going to write down some instructions in case that happens. You know the drill. They get worse before they get better."

"I do know. Thanks, Doc." He held out his hand for the instructions. "And thanks for the heads-up about Mariah."

Doc Miller frowned. "Not a problem, but I hope you don't mind me saying this. Watch out. You know how political things can get. All it takes is for one of your jocks to do something one of the other trainers doesn't like and they'll pounce. You don't want to get in a situation where your livelihood is in jeopardy because of who you're dating."

Was that a threat? Or just a warning? "Point taken."

"Good."

But as Doc Miller walked back to his track-side office, it was hard for Zach to battle back his irritation. The doctor knew everyone, and if people were talking, it must be pretty serious if he was bringing it to Zach's attention.

He debated whether or not to tell Mariah, but he didn't want to tell her about Doc Miller's visit. Worse, he wasn't entirely certain he bought the good doctor's diagnosis. He'd never second-guessed the man before, but telling him to race a hurting horse just didn't sit well.

"Hey," Mariah said when she saw him later that day, and the way she looked up at him and smiled, the way her eyes lit up, it caused his heart to soften and his whole damn body to tingle.

He'd caught her standing behind the reception area, one of her coworkers eyeing him up and down.

"Hey," he replied. But there was something else in her eyes, too. Fear? Anxiety? Uncertainty?

"You're early, not that it matters. I know I said we

could work on Dasher, but we just had a client haul a horse in. She's in foal and she thinks something's wrong."

"I can come back later."

She appeared to consider, but then she shook her head. "Why don't you come on back with me? As many mares as you've helped foal out, you might come in handy."

She motioned him toward the back of the clinic, and Zach smiled at the dark-haired receptionist who'd been eyeing him earlier. The place was so cavernous his footsteps echoed through the room. Behind the granite-topped front desk was a mural of horses running. Doors were set on either side of it. He'd learned the other day the one to the left led to exam rooms for small animals and the one to the right led to the equine surgery center, followed by the stalls. The mare stood in the surgery center, her sides bloated from foal, head hanging low. She was a bay, but her brown coat looked nearly as black as her mane in spots thanks to her sweat. He could tell she was in labor by her rapid breathing.

"When is she due?" Mariah asked the owner, a frightened-looking woman with short blond hair.

"Not for two weeks."

Mariah had pulled her hair back, and Zach noted she appeared very doctorlike in her white lab coat. "Well, she's definitely in labor. Has her water broken?"

"I don't think so. She's in a stall and I didn't see anything."

The owner glanced at the mare in concern. Clearly she had run her hands through her hair more than a few times. Her T-shirt looked as though she'd slept in it and if he didn't miss his guess, those were manure stains on her pant legs.

"What's her name?" Mariah walked up to the mare,

pulling a stethoscope from her pocket and placing it against the mare's sides.

"Belle."

"She is *bella,*" Mariah said with an easy smile. "Is this her first foal?"

"First for us both." The woman patted the horse's neck, her eyes growing soft as she gazed into her eyes.

"That's probably part of the problem. Maiden mares can be tricky. Let's see what we've got going on. Cami, can you get me a glove?"

A woman Zach hadn't even noticed came forward. Judging by her smock, she was clearly the vet tech. She moved to a cabinet, removing a box and some jelly. Zach always hated to watch this part, but he knew it was necessary, and to be honest, he was kind of fascinated by Dr. Mariah. She was all business as she snapped the latex over her arm and he found himself thinking she was a really good vet. She kept giving the owner reassuring smiles, and she spoke kindly to the mare as she began her investigation.

"Oh, yeah," she said. "She's foaling, and she's breech. You're lucky her water hasn't broken yet. We'll have to turn it before she can give birth, but I'll need everyone's help.

"Mary," she said to the owner, "the foaling stall is the last stall on the left. Go ahead and take her in. Cami, can you get me the pullers? Zach, let's get some gloves on you. I may need your manly strength to help me turn the foal."

"My manly strength," he said with a smile. "I like the sound of that."

She smiled, and he kind of liked the way her eyes lit up when he made her grin, but then she put on her professional face and she oozed confidence as she helped him scrub up. Her can-do attitude completely mesmerized him. Who was this woman? And why did he find himself wanting to kiss her?

"Let's go."

The mare was so distressed that she seemed oblivious to her surroundings. Even Dasher's soft nicker from a few stalls down didn't faze her. She barely lifted her head when they entered the stall. Mariah went up to her and patted her neck, and Zach heard her murmur something soothing before turning to the group at large.

"Cami, I'll need you to hold her tail. Zach, you *have* done this before, haven't you?"

"More times than I can count."

"Perfect. I'm going to reach in and move the foal's head. Hopefully, that will help nature take its course, but if I don't have the strength to do it, Zach, I may need you to jump in."

"No problem," he said.

She went right back to business. Zach stood by as she went about lubing up her gloves. It wasn't as easy as it might look to simply reach inside and move a foal's head. Sometimes it took a great deal of strength to push the foal back into the uterus so it could present the correct way—front legs first. Within minutes he knew the foal wasn't cooperating, because he could see Mariah's frown of impatience. She tried one angle, then the next, then another still. He was right on the verge of offering to help her out when her eyes lit up and she said, "There. Geez." She withdrew her hand. "Stubborn little bugger."

"Will she be okay?" Zach asked.

"I think so." She tossed her gloves in the garbage outside the stall. "If she was full term I'd offer to break her water now, but let's see what happens."

"Oh! Thank goodness," Mary gushed. "I was so afraid the foal would be stillborn."

"Not even close. Little guy was kicking around in there. That's what made it so hard. Kept jerking his head. Plus, she's contracting pretty hard. I'm thinking she's going to definitely deliver tonight, but let's just leave her alone and see what happens. You can kick back in the reception area if you want, or your vehicle. We'll keep an eye on her through the foaling camera. If her contractions become more intense, we'll let you know."

"I'd rather wait outside her stall."

"How about in the exam area instead? Sometimes mares get shy when they know a human's around."

Mary's smile was pure relief. "Sounds good to me."

"Foal's a good size," Mariah said as they walked back to the exam area. "If she does deliver tonight, I have no doubt it'll do just fine."

Mary had tears in her eyes. "I can't thank you enough, Dr. Stewart." She gave Mariah a hug. "I was so worried."

Mariah hugged Mary back. "My pleasure. Welcoming a new foal into the world is part of what I love about my job."

The two women laughed and it was then, right then, as he watched kindness fill Mariah's eyes, that Zach began to fall in love.

Chapter Seventeen

Something was up.

As they watched the Cool Jet go to work on Dasher's leg, Zach kept sneaking glances at her. It got to the point that she started to grow self-conscious until she just couldn't take it anymore.

"What *is* it?"

"What?" He stared at her in question, blinked. "Oh, nothing."

"Bull." She crossed her arms in front of her. "Something's bothering you."

His eyes skated over Dasher's black coat, down to his legs, up to his head. "All right, fine." He swiped a hand over his face. "I have a confession to make."

She tensed. She had no idea what he was about to say, but she was pretty certain it was tied in to her work with Belle earlier. He'd been staring at her strangely ever since she'd repositioned the foal.

"What?"

He opened his mouth, closed it, then blurted, "I had Dr. Miller look at one of the horses I'm training today."

For some reason she didn't think that was what he'd been about to say. "So?"

"So? I thought you might be offended."

She let him see her amusement. "What? Like you're cheating on me or something?"

She could tell he tried not to smile. "Something like that." But then he lost it, laughing.

She shook her head. "Zach, you can call whatever vet you want."

He appeared so relieved it made her smile again. "He did mention something that concerned me, though. It seems a bunch of the guys have been talking. They think you're some kind of spy or something and that you have an ulterior motive for dating me. Something to do with videotaping racehorses being abused."

All trace of a smile vanished. "So they already know about us."

"They do."

Thanks, Wes.

"And they think I'm using you to expose the dark side of racing."

"Something like that."

"You have *got* to be kidding me."

"Wish I was."

"You don't believe that, do you?"

"After watching you with that mare's owner, I don't think there's a malicious bone in your body."

She relaxed. "There's not."

"I know." And there it was again, that look he kept giving her, the one that made her think there was more to his words than he was letting on. "You're one of the most amazing women I've ever met."

And now she was the one having to look away lest he read too much into her own eyes. She loved that he saw her that way. It made her feel…special. She cleared her throat. "What was wrong with your horse?"

"Stone bruise? He thinks. Not sure."

"Did he take X-rays? Block him? Hoof testers?"

"Hoof testers, but that's it."

"Then how does he know it's a stone bruise?"

"He doesn't. It's his best guess."

"Guess? Are you kidding?"

"I know, I know." Zach held up his hands. "But Dr. Miller has seen a lot of stone bruises over the years, so it's probably a good guess."

She examined his face. "But you're not convinced."

He shook his head. "Not really."

"Why not?"

"I don't know. Just the way he's moving."

She glanced down at the Cool Jet, watching as it deflated only to have ice-cold water pump into the boot a second later. Dasher looked superbly unfazed by it all.

"Do you need me to look at him?"

"I don't want to impose."

"Zach, you wouldn't be imposing."

"Dr. Stewart! Belle just went down."

Mary peeked her head around the edge of the barn aisle. "Should I go check on her?"

"Hold on." Mariah smiled in Mary's direction, then glanced down at Dasher's leg. "Why don't you unhook him? I'll go look at the mare through the foal cam."

It took only one glance and Mariah could tell the time had come. "Her water just broke. See?" She pointed to the monitor where a wet spot could be seen in the shavings. "Looks like we're going to have a baby tonight."

"Really?" the owner said. "I thought she was just going to the bathroom. Oh, my gosh. I've got to call my husband."

"Better tell him to get here soon." She headed back

for Zach and Dasher. He was just pulling off the boot. "Put him away. We've got a foal coming."

"Hey, that's great."

"I'm going to go take a peek and make sure the foal didn't twist again."

She ran to get gloves. Mary was at her mare's head when she entered the stall.

"She's breathing heavily." Mary's eyes were filled with fear. "And I think that's the amniotic sac back there?"

"Yup. That's it. The start of it, at least."

The mare groaned. Mariah quickly moved to the horse's rear, relieved to see two front feet encased in the gossamer-white sac. "I see legs now."

Mary looked panic-stricken. "Already?"

"It's okay. Sometimes it happens quickly, sometimes not."

"Can I watch?"

"Of course."

"I won't be in the way?"

"Not at all," Mariah said with a laugh. "Come on."

Zach came into the stall, his face lighting up when he spotted the legs. "Looks like you fixed the breech."

"Looks like it."

"Should we help pull or something?" the owner asked.

"No. Not unless she needs help, but she's doing just fine on her own."

"Sorry," Mary said. "I've been doing some reading, but I thought I'd have another two weeks to bone up. I feel so stupid."

"It's okay." Mariah rested a hand on the woman's shoulder. "That's what we're here for." She included Zach in her smile. "Zach breeds racehorses. He's probably seen more foals born than anyone at the clinic."

"Really? Wow."

Just then the mare groaned again, her sides seeming to spasm as she gave another huge push. More of the foal's legs emerged, up to its knees, as did the tip of a tiny muzzle.

"Oh, my goodness," she heard Mary squeak.

"It's a sorrel," Zach observed.

"Two white socks," Mariah added.

"I wish my husband was here," Mary murmured.

Mariah felt something brush her hand. A moment later Zach's fingers entwined with her own. She glanced at him in surprise, and the warmth in his smile made her breath catch and her heart stop beating for a moment. He felt it, too, that sense of wonder and magic that seemed to fill the air whenever an animal gave birth. She could see it in his eyes. She squeezed his hand back. He didn't let go and that was okay because she wanted him to hold on to her.

Another push and this time the whole head emerged. The shoulders came next, the three of them rooting the mare on. At some point Mary's husband arrived, and the woman burst into tears.

"I thought you were going to miss it," she cried.

"I drove like a maniac to get here in time," said a dark-haired man with the look of someone who made his living out of doors. Big, burly, but with kind eyes. "If you hear sirens outside, it's just the cop that was chasing me."

"Simon!" The woman swatted him, but she was laughing.

A half hour later they all watched, breathless, Mariah still holding Zach's hand, as the tiny foal broke free of the amniotic sac. Mariah moved forward to clear the foal's tiny nose of mucus, relieved to see that he or she was already breathing. The foal shifted, tearing the sac more, and Mariah smiled up at Mary.

"It's a boy."

"Is it!" Mary gave a little squeal. "We were hoping for a boy."

The tiny horse lifted its head. In the next moment it tried to stand, failed and tried again. Everyone held their breath, the mare sitting up, too, and nickering at her baby as if encouraging it to try one more time.

"She knows," Mary said. "She knows that's her baby."

They always knew. Mariah's eyes heated with unshed tears. She was such a sap. She couldn't watch a foal being born without getting all choked up, especially when the mare stood up a moment later, the new mom nuzzling her baby and nickering again. When Mariah glanced at Zach, she spotted the same look of tender joy as she no doubt sported. This man, someone who'd seen perhaps hundreds of births in his lifetime, could still be moved by the process—as could she.

He caught her looking at him. She smiled. He smiled back, bending and giving her a gentle kiss.

"Beautiful," he said softly.

"It is."

"No," he said, touching the side of her face. "You're beautiful."

THEY LEFT THE CLINIC an hour later, mama and baby doing great. Zach told himself not to push spending the night with her again, but when they got back to her place, Mariah invited him to stay. One thing led to another and they ended up making love. Something had changed between them, though. Perhaps it was witnessing the miracle of life, but their lovemaking seemed more intense, more passionate than ever before.

He awoke the next morning confused about where he was.

Mariah's tiny apartment, he suddenly recalled.

The sun was just coming up. Zach rolled over and spied Mariah next to him. She lay there completely oblivious to the world and as he thought about the competent, caring woman she'd been the evening before, his heart did an odd little flip. He could get used to this, he admitted, used to waking up next to her. The thought should have scared the crap out of him. He'd never been a big believer in long-term relationships. Suddenly, however, he could understand the appeal.

He kissed Mariah awake. And when her eyes didn't open right away, he kissed her neck, then her ear.

"Mmm," she moaned.

"Wake up, love," he said softly. "Busy day."

He pulled back, pleased to note her eyes were open. In the near darkness her hair looked almost brown and she had so much of it, it looked as if she lay on a pillow of hair. He shoved a stray lock of it out of her eyes as she stared up at him. He had a feeling she studied his face.

"You're still here."

"Of course."

She glanced toward her kitchen, the place where she lived the size of a foaling stall, so it wasn't far away.

"What time is it?"

"Six something." He could have sworn she frowned. This time he studied her. "Worried what your friends might think?"

Her pupils flared. "No. Of course not. I just don't want to be late to work."

"You won't be."

He tried kissing her again. She wouldn't let him. "What's wrong?"

"Nothing," she said.

"Baloney." He swiped another lock of hair out of her eyes.

Her lashes swept down. "I just don't know where this is headed."

"And that scares you?"

She didn't answer.

"Because you should know it scares the shit out of me."

Brown eyes jerked back to his own.

"So let's just take this slow, okay? That way, neither one of us does something stupid."

Her eyes darted around his face, seeming to search every inch of it. What she saw must have reassured her, because she said, "Okay."

He smiled at her again before rolling out of her tiny bed and grabbing his clothes. "I almost hate to ask, but do you think you'd mind looking at that horse I told you about last night?"

"Why would I mind?"

He glanced back at her, pulling on his jeans. "I don't want you to think I'm using you."

"Aren't I the one that's supposedly using you?"

"I know. Ironic, isn't it?"

"Bring him in this afternoon. I'll text you a time when I get into work."

"Sounds good."

He left before he lost his willpower and did something that would result in both of them being late, but he found himself whistling on his way home and then later on his way to work.

It was a good thing he had Mariah's visit to look forward to, because his day turned to shit the minute he got to the track. Apparently someone had told one of his best clients that he was seeing Mariah and it didn't sit well with the man that Zach was dating "that damned animal-rights activist." The man threatened to pull his horses out of training. Zach told him to go ahead, and that was that but the loss of him would put another dent in Zach's finances. He tried not to think about it too much when he went to get Cash out of his stall so he could take him to see Mariah. Honestly, he'd be glad to get away. Judging by the looks on some of his fellow trainers' faces, word had definitely gotten out that he was dating the enemy.

His cell phone interrupted him.

"It's me," Mariah said. "Don't come right now. I have a farm call not far from the track. I could swing by afterward."

His stomach tightened at the mere thought of her showing up at his work, especially given some of the hostile stares he'd been receiving. But then he told himself he was being ridiculous. His peers might not like Mariah, but they'd never be overtly rude to her, not while he was around. She'd be okay.

"Sure. Come by whenever."

He couldn't shake the feeling, however, that bringing her to the track would be a mistake. Didn't matter how many times he told himself otherwise.

The feeling only grew worse when Wes showed up, his usual smile firmly in place when he said, "I hear you're going to be the doom of us all."

Zach looked up from the feed instructions he'd been writing down. "Don't tell me you've heard the rumors, too?"

Wes's green eyes were full of amusement. "Yup. I hear she's gathering intel on us all. We're all going to be on *60 Minutes* when she blows the lid off horse racing in her tell-all."

"You're kidding."

Wes lifted his hands, his smile growing even more amused. "Wish I was."

Zach glanced around, spotting one of the trainers who'd glared at him earlier in the day—Manny Diaz.

"I say let them sweat. I trust your judgment. They should, too."

Zach ran his hands through his hair. "The problem is she's coming here this afternoon."

Wes's eyebrows shot up. "You invited the enemy?"

"She's looking at Cash."

"I thought Dr. Miller already did that."

"He did, but I asked Mariah for a second opinion."

"When's she coming?"

Zach glanced at his cell phone. "Any minute now."

"Right on. I'm sticking around to watch the fireworks."

"It won't be that bad."

"Maybe you'll get lucky and they'll refuse to let her in."

"Wes—"

The rest of what he'd been about to say was interrupted by the sound of a diesel engine. Everyone in the vicinity turned, but no one gave the white veterinary truck a second glance. It wasn't until Mariah slipped out, her bright red hair instantly visible, that he saw a few heads turn.

"She's a vet?" he thought he heard someone ask.

"Oh, yeah," Wes said. "This'll be interesting."

Chapter Eighteen

Mariah froze the minute she got out of the clinic's truck. "What?" she asked Zach and Wes, who were both staring at her. She smiled at Wes in greeting, the man grinning back in a way that made her instantly suspicious. "What's going on?"

"We're waiting for the lynch mob to form," Wes said.

"Oh." She smiled and shook her head.

"Ignore him," Zach said, smiling, too, but it was a forced grin. "Glad you could make it. Cash's right here." He walked to a bay horse's stall. "He still looked off to me this morning, but it's no worse than before."

"Bring him on out," Mariah told Zach, admiring the beautiful stallion he led forward. She went up to him and held her hand out. "Hey there, son."

"Do you want me to trot him?"

Mariah shook her head. "Just walk him forward, then turn him sharply to the right."

Zach's row of stalls had an overhang and he set off beneath it, the other horses in the stalls peering out at him, some of them moving forward so they could get a better look. When Zach made a sudden turn to the right, she could see instantly what he meant by the horse stepping oddly.

"Okay, same thing but to the left."

When he headed back toward her, Mariah looked past the stallion and straight into the eyes of a man who clearly wasn't happy to see her. Manny Diaz. She recognized him from her protests in the past. Big, dark and with a temper. He'd always made it clear he didn't like her. Based on the rumors she'd heard about him drugging horses, she didn't much like him, either.

Zach turned the gelding toward her and she could tell immediately the horse was more sore on the inside right wall than the outside.

"Okay, come on back." The horse's ears perked up as they headed toward his stall and beneath the shade of the overhang. "I see what you mean about being sore. He's not dead lame, but he's definitely favoring that leg when he moves from side to side."

There was some swelling, too, above the coronet band near the top of the hoof. Not unheard of with a festering abscess but still troubling, especially since the official diagnosis had leaned toward a stone bruise.

"Let's take some film, if you don't mind." She glanced at Wes. "Maybe you can help me out while Zach holds the horse. We were shorthanded when I left, so I don't have an assistant today."

"Not a problem."

When she went back to her truck, she glanced down the barn aisle. Manny had been joined by another man and they were very clearly talking about her.

She returned with the portable X-ray machine as well as the film and the block of wood she had horses stand on, but the whole time she set things up, she could feel eyes boring into the back of her head. She knew Zach saw it, too. He shot her a reassuring smile, but she felt like the reptile in a petting zoo. Thank goodness everything was digitized, which made the process quick and easy.

"There it is." She motioned for Zach and Wes to come to the back of her truck, where her laptop was open on the tailgate. "Look. See this? His coffin bone is chipped."

"Son of a—" Zach still held Cash's lead rope and he glanced back at the horse as if silently reproaching the horse for his injury.

"I'll be," Wes said. "Gotta admit, looked like a stone bruise to me."

Mariah shook her head. "Usually with a stone bruise they're sore all the time, but he was stepping funny only when he moved a certain way."

"Thank God I didn't race him."

And there it was, the reminder of what he did for a living and how destructive it could be. She was glad he wouldn't be racing Dasher again once the horse had healed. "You would have raced him?"

"No, but Doc Miller told me it would be okay if we did, but I disagreed. I was going to suggest to the owner that we give him time off."

And here was a reminder that he wasn't like the other owners and trainers. He cared.

"It's lucky you didn't." She turned her attention back to the horse. "The good news is he'll likely make a full recovery. The biggest concern is infection, but if we start him on a course of antibiotics, he should be fine."

Manny was walking by. They all three looked up. Mariah wasn't surprised to spot his glare, but the man's brown eyes slid over her in such a way that she shivered.

"Manny," she heard Zach call out to the man in greeting.

The trainer shot them all a glare.

"Whew. You could fry an egg with that death ray," Wes said.

"He hates me," Mariah said softly.

"They *all* hate you."

Mariah glanced at Wes sharply. "Well, not me. I have better taste than they do. And not Zach, but you should hear them talking."

"What else are they saying?" Zach asked quickly.

Wes shrugged. "That she's using her good looks to get you into her bed. That she'll dump you the moment she manages to make us all look bad. That she burns children at the stake."

Mariah wasn't surprised. What did surprise her, however, was the ferociousness in Zach's eyes.

"Well, you can tell them from me that they're all wrong. All Mariah wants to do is help horses. She'll do whatever it takes to accomplish that, including helping me. She's never charged me a dime for her services. She only wants to help. Tell them that."

She wanted to hug Zach, she really did. She felt her cheeks color, but it wasn't out of embarrassment or discomfort. Her cheeks flushed because suddenly she wanted to cry.

"Hey, it's not me that has the problem," Wes said, lifting his hands.

Zach *got* her, Mariah thought. He really, really got her.

"I know." Zach shook his head. "They just drive me crazy with their closed-minded thinking."

Mariah glanced up at Zach, a sense of pride filling her. Her whole body glowed with warmth and happiness and something that felt like…

Love?

She took a deep breath. Whatever it was, she'd never felt anything like it.

"I would just ignore them," Wes said. "They'll learn."

"They will," Zach said. Then he glanced down at her. "Come on. Let's finish up."

You've been seduced by the dark side. Jillian's words echoed in her head.

And she finally admitted that she had been.

THEY WERE INSEPARABLE from that day forward. Mariah still avoided the track even though he told her she had nothing to hide. As they worked to get Dasher and then Summer sound, she seemed to come to terms with what he did for a living even if she refused to go to his "office."

The day of her meeting with the board of directors, he was just as nervous as she was, but nothing had ever made him more proud than when she stood up in front of her fellow CEASE members and the board of directors and gave her speech about forming an animal-welfare league. Since he was in a relationship with Mariah, he opted out of the vote, but he needn't have worried. The board unanimously agreed to get behind her idea. Even her friend Jillian seemed to approve.

"That's a step in the right direction," Jillian said afterward, but when her gaze caught on him, her expression changed. "Considering."

Considering what?

"I know," Mariah said. "Considering they're evil racehorse owners."

Jillian laughed, hugging her friend.

But the woman's smile faded behind Mariah's back. Her eyes spoke to Zach and Zach alone.

You hurt her, and I'll kill you.

He nodded. She stepped back. "I'll see you at the Grand Prix this weekend, right?"

"Yeah, sure."

Jillian smiled. "Good. I'll see you there."

The woman walked away without another backward glance.

"She doesn't approve of us," Mariah admitted softly.

"She'll get over it."

That night they made love with a tenderness that left Mariah in tears. Zach had never thought about marriage before, not after watching his parents destroy each other, but for the first time he found himself wanting to spend the rest of his life with one person. She'd become his best friend, someone he could talk to about his fears of losing the ranch, who hugged him when he'd had a bad day and who shared his love of horses. The only fly in the ointment was her unwillingness to have anything to do with his horse-racing business. Still. It wasn't a deal breaker. She worked diligently with Dasher—with great results—so much so that Zach was beginning to wonder if perhaps they *could* race him.

"So what do you think?" he asked as he trotted Dasher one last time along the side of the vet clinic's stabling area. It'd been two months since she'd taken over his care. Two months of painstaking therapy and exercise, all of which had resulted in a horse that hadn't taken an off step in weeks. She'd helped Summer, too. They'd injected the filly with a fluid that had helped to build more soft tissue in the bones of her foot, and it had worked.

"He looks good."

He halted the horse, walking beneath an access road lined by walnut trees. "What did his ultrasound look like?"

"Amazingly clean." But she didn't seem as pleased by the news as Zach might have expected. "I even had Dr. Saffer give them a look. He agrees. It's hard to tell he ever had an injury."

"Good enough to race?"

It was as if she'd just given him a diagnosis of terminal cancer, he admitted, and he knew why.

"Zach, we talked about this weeks ago. It's not a good idea to race him."

"I know, but he's doing so good. You told me yourself he's as good as new."

"Not good enough to race."

He disagreed. He'd seen the X-rays and the ultrasound. Not only was his injury healed, she'd said herself the leg was probably even stronger than it had been before.

"I'm not going to race him, not right away. I just want to haul him to the track. Give him a test run."

But she didn't want him to. He saw her take a deep breath. She stood in a patch of sunlight, her troubled face perfectly illuminated. When her brown eyes met his own, they were filled with hurt. "You promised me you wouldn't."

"I never promised." He took a deep breath, too. "Okay, maybe I implied he wouldn't be raced, but I honestly didn't think he'd get better. If I had, maybe I'd have made my intentions more clear, but even you said he was ready to ride again."

"There's a difference between riding and racing."

"You mean to tell me what Dandy's doing is somehow less risky than what Dasher does on the track?"

"I didn't say that."

"Well, is it?"

She didn't want to answer him and he knew he'd raised a good point. Still, he softened his tone.

"Mariah, I'm not going to push him. I'll let him stretch out a bit and see how he does. Nothing big. If he gets sore, we'll go back to plan A."

"Sore? What if he tears it again? This time catastrophically? What if he ends up permanently lame? Do you care that he might live out the rest of his life in pain?"

"Couldn't he do that jumping?"

"That's different. Hunter/jumper people take better care of their horses."

He couldn't believe she would say such a thing. Then again, he could. He glanced at Dasher, the animal's black coat looking spotted beneath the light of the trees. It was as if he stood on a piece of earth, one that suddenly opened up, a wide chasm separating the two of them.

He slowly shook his head. "My family has spent decades trying to breed horses like Dasher and Summer and Dandy. Years. You're asking me to throw it all away, to potentially lose everything my family has worked for, because there's a chance Dasher might hurt himself."

She never wavered when she said, "I am."

"That's insane."

She flinched. "How so?"

"Mariah, every time I send a horse out to race, every time, there's a chance they could get hurt."

"I know. That's why I can't watch it."

"Do you watch car racing?"

She appeared momentarily confused. "It's not the same thing."

"All right, how about football?"

"I don't watch sports."

"Ice-skating?" He lifted a brow. "Come on, you have to admit, that hardly qualifies as a sport."

She didn't soften her stance. Not a little bit. "I know where you're going with this, but it's not the same. Animals are defenseless. They can't tell you if they're hurting or sore or scared. It's up to us as human beings to guard them from injury."

"By padding them with Bubble Wrap?"

He could see the frustration in her eyes. "That's not what I'm saying."

Dasher tugged on the lead rope, and Zach looked back in time to see the stallion stretch toward a patch of grass lining the gravel road. What she asked for was impossible. If both Mariah and her boss thought Dasher's injury had healed, then that was good enough for him—no matter what she might think.

"I'm going to put him back in training."

"Don't."

"I have to."

"Then I can't be a part of it."

His whole body went on alert. "What are you saying?"

She lifted her chin. "If you do this, you're not the man I thought you were."

Chapter Nineteen

He thought she was crazy, Mariah realized. His look said it all.

"I'm exactly the man you think I am. I just don't see the difference between jumping a horse and racing them."

"There's a world of difference."

He ran a hand through his hair. "Look, can we just discuss this later?"

It would be so easy to do that. So nice to postpone the inevitable. "I was talking to Jillian the other day."

"Jillian." He shook his head. "That woman hates me."

"She doesn't hate you. She just hates what you do for a living."

"Same thing."

And there was the crux of the problem, she conceded. Zach and racing were interchangeable. Parts of the same whole. Inseparable. She'd been fooling herself over the past few weeks. He wasn't different. The proof stood in front of her.

"Jillian told me the only way anything will ever change in your industry is if someone like you changes the way things are done. You have to stop putting horses' lives at risk." She took a step toward him. "Zach, she's right. You have to know that racing Dasher is a huge risk. If something goes wrong—"

"Nothing will go wrong."

He didn't get it. She sighed in frustration. "Come here."

She didn't wait to see if he would follow, just turned toward the entrance to the clinic. The sound of Dasher's hooves was her only clue that he'd done as she asked.

"Wait here."

It seemed dark inside, but the fluorescent lights overhead helped her to spot her laptop lying on the counter of the exam room. She opened it, searching for one file in particular.

"Look," she said, clicking on a button. She took Dasher's lead from him, guiding the stallion toward his open stall not far from the exam area.

"What is it?" he called out after her.

"What do you think it is?" she asked as she turned the horse loose.

When she returned to the hospital area, he peered down at the screen, frowning. "It looks like a horse's leg."

"That's right. A cannon bone."

"Are those screws holding it together?"

"That's exactly what they are."

He turned toward her with dismay. "Mariah, these things happen. Hell, they happen to people—"

"They're going to race him that way."

To give him credit, his expression turned horrified. "What?"

"They're Thoroughbred owners. The horse races down at Santa Anita and there's a big purse next month. When Dr. Saffer told them the bone had healed, they were delighted. They bragged about how they could now race him. They didn't care that the animal might break down in the middle of a race. Didn't give a damn about the jockey that might be injured should the horse stumble and fall once the leg broke in two. All they cared about was the purse money."

"Mariah," he said softly, all traces of irritation gone. "You know I'm not like that."

"Aren't you?"

He flinched. "Dasher's injury is nowhere near as catastrophic."

"It could be."

"He's not going to break a leg."

"How do you know?"

"Because I know horses."

"You're not a vet."

She saw him bite back some words, watched him take a deep breath, and when she looked deep in his eyes, she spotted something close to panic there. "This is ridiculous," he muttered.

"Not to me."

"I think we both need to calm down—"

"I'm not bending on this issue, Zach. All my friends at CEASE know I've been working toward getting Dasher sound. I'll look like a hypocrite if you race him again."

"And I don't see the point of keeping an animal from doing something he's been bred to do."

"And I do."

"So what are you saying?"

Her gaze didn't waver even though inside she quaked with fear. "I'm not saying anything. I'm asking you, Zach. Please, don't race him again. Please."

He didn't move. Didn't blink. He'd gone pale. She saw his hands clench. "Mariah—"

"You're going to do it, aren't you?"

"I have to."

"No, you don't."

"I have to at least try."

"Then I guess that's it."

"No." He reached for her.

She stepped back. "I can't, Zach. I can't watch you do it." Even if she wouldn't actually physically be there when he raced, she would know. Just as she'd known when he raced his horses in the past. She'd just turned a blind eye to it, but she couldn't do that anymore. Jillian was right. She'd gone to the dark side and all because she'd fallen in love.

You're not in love.

Wasn't she, though? Wasn't that why this hurt so dang much?

"Look, let's talk this over later." He tried touching her again. This time she let him pull her into his arms.

You are not *in love.*

"We can have dinner at my place," she heard him say. "Talk it over after we've both had time to think about it." He leaned back, looked into her eyes. "I'll call you later on."

She wouldn't change her mind. She tried to tell him that with her eyes.

"I'll send someone over to pick up Dasher later today."

Her head bowed. He didn't get it after all. Despite what she'd thought the other day, he didn't get *her.*

When he tipped her chin up, she had the damnedest time keeping the tears from her eyes.

"I'll see you later," he said tenderly.

No, he wouldn't.

"So I DID the right thing, right?"

Jillian nodded from her position at the kitchen table. Mariah grabbed a pillow from her couch and hugged it to her. The same couch where she and Zach had—

She shuttered the thought.

"I mean, I was an *idiot* for assuming he wouldn't race Dasher again."

"You know what they say about ass-uming," Jillian said. Her friend tried to smile, but it came out looking more like a Halloween-mask grin. "I'm glad you set him straight."

"The thing is, Jillian, I know he loves horses. I mean, I could never be with a man that didn't."

"Apparently, he doesn't love them enough."

But he did. *He did,* she wanted to scream.

"What'd you do when he came to get Dasher?"

"I pretended I was on a call." She fiddled with a loose string on the edge of the pillow, tugged on it in the hopes of tearing it off. The seam started to fray, the piping coming loose.

Like my life.

"That was smart," Jillian said, her short dark hair mussed, no doubt due to Mariah's panicked call and her pleas to come to Uptown Farms as soon as she could. Clearly, she hadn't taken time to brush her hair.

"He'll change his mind." Mariah refused to believe otherwise. "When I give him the cold shoulder for a few days, he'll get the point."

When Jillian didn't say anything, Mariah looked up.

"And if he doesn't?" her friend asked.

"He will."

But Jillian didn't appear convinced. Mariah told herself to ignore her dour look of pessimism. It would all work out.

Still, as the evening came to a close and she ignored all ten of Zach's phone calls, she found herself covering her head with a pillow and screaming. It was the hardest thing in the world to give him the silent treatment. Worse, she missed him. It amazed her how quickly she'd gotten used to having him around. It wasn't just the sex, either. She missed the daily rundown of how their days had gone. Missed sharing a meal with him. Missed the laughter.

He stopped by the clinic the next day. She'd anticipated the move, so she'd asked the girls to schedule her on farm calls. Driving between the different stables gave her lots of time to think, the knot in her stomach doubling in size when she saw the number of missed calls on her cell.

He was waiting for her when she got back later that night.

She probably could have avoided him. They parked the clinic trucks around the back and she could have driven like a maniac and gotten there before him, but she couldn't avoid him forever.

"How's Dasher?" she asked the moment she slipped out of the truck.

"Why haven't you been returning my calls?"

He was hurt. She could see it in his eyes. Honestly, she didn't blame him. She might not like what he did for a living, but she hated manipulating him even more. That was what it felt as if she was doing—trying to force his hand. It didn't sit well with her. Not at all.

"I needed time to think."

He looked so handsome standing there. He'd come

straight from the track, his standard-issue jeans, cowboy hat and red polo peppered by small specks of dirt. Clearly, he'd been splashed by mud at some point during the day. It didn't look as if he cared.

"And?" he prompted.

"Nothing's changed, Zach."

And it made her sick. Despite what she'd told Jillian last night, she worried—no, she very much *feared*—there was no way around the matter.

"Dasher or you."

She hadn't thought of it that way, but she guessed that was what it boiled down to. "Sort of."

"That's blackmail."

"I—" She opened her mouth to deny it, but she couldn't. Suddenly, the fight drained out of her. It left her weak. She leaned against the driver's-side door of the truck. "It's not just Dasher. It's the three young colts you have at the ranch, too. I'm going to have to watch you saddle and bridle and break them at some point in the future. And what about when one of them is horribly injured? If not Dasher, then some other horse of yours. It'll happen, and I'll be forced to fix it, only don't you see, I'll feel as if I'm enabling you. As if I somehow condone what you're doing, and I just wouldn't be able to live with myself."

"So you're willing to throw everything we have away…to simply pack up and leave. No compromise. No trying to make it work. Just toss it all away like my mom and my dad."

"No." She took a step toward him. "Not like that. I'm not like your mom at all."

Far from appeasing him, he suddenly looked incensed. "Do you realize that I'm in love with you?"

She almost sagged against the door again.

"I fell in love with you the day you delivered that foal. I was going to surprise you. I was going to drag you to a race and ask you to marry me in front of the entire crowd."

He took a step toward her. "I love you, Mariah. I love you so much it hurts, and this…this *thing* you ask of me, it's wrong."

Good Lord, was he serious?

"I can't do this." She tried to walk away.

He wouldn't let her go. "This is my livelihood you're talking about. Not just mine, but everyone I employ. And it's the legacy my dad built. It's the future I've been trying to create. Please, for the love of God, don't ask me to keep a horse off the track when he deserves a chance to run. Not when I'm so close. Not when a horse could break a leg running out in a pasture. Or jumping. Or stepping out of a trailer wrong."

She flinched.

"Please, Mariah."

She couldn't. She just couldn't. "I'm sorry, Zach."

Those were tears in her eyes. They didn't fall, but they were there nonetheless, hovering near her lashes.

"You're a hypocrite, Mariah. If you think I'm bad, you need to call your friends who jump horses bad, too. And the people that *rescue* horses at auction and then barrel race them, they are evil, too. You should protest a barrel race. Hell, while you're at it, go after the reining people and the cutting-horse people, too. Anyone that dares to give their horse a job, one that involves physical labor, that's who you need to go after. Don't just go after me."

"That's different."

"Is it, Mariah? Is it really?"

It was. They didn't do half the horrible things the racing industry did to their horses.

Right?

She brushed the thought away. He was just playing with her mind, that was all. Horse-show people treated their horses like glass.

Not all of them.

"Goodbye, Mariah."

She opened eyes she hadn't even known she'd closed and the minute she did, she wished she'd close them again. So much pain ebbed from his blue eyes, so much sadness and regret, it nearly killed her.

"Dasher came off the track sound. I'm increasing his work schedule. There's a race next month. Not here, down south. A big one. I think Dasher has a shot. If it's the only race you ever watch in your life, Mariah, let it be that one. It's televised. You can watch it at home. You've worked so hard to get Dasher to where he is today—I want you to watch him run. I want you to look at him when he does. To see the pride he takes in his job. To watch him hold his head high and prance to the gate in anticipation of what he was born to do. He loves it, Mariah, and I swear to you, he wants to run. He wants to race. Don't take that away from him."

A tear ran down her cheek. She could feel the hot trail until it dropped off the side of her jaw. Somehow he'd approached without her knowing. All she felt was the soft brush of his hand on her cheek.

"Take care of yourself."

And when he drove away a few minutes later, she knew it was for the last time.

Chapter Twenty

He didn't call her.

She'd known he wouldn't. He'd made it clear he wouldn't. Still, a part of her had hoped....

Stupid.

And to what end? she asked herself. What if he *did* call? Had anything changed? She refused to align herself with an industry that caused the death of two horses for every one thousand horses that raced. And that was just in the Thoroughbred industry. What if they combined stats from the other breeds? Horrible. Their relationship had been doomed from the start. Deep down she'd known that. It was why she'd refused to fall in love with him.

Still, as the days flew by, she wondered how Dasher was doing. The clinic had gotten a bunch of referrals from some of Zach's friends. Each time a trainer or an owner came in, she wanted to ask how the stallion was doing. She assumed he was doing well based on the calls they were getting asking about their treatment plan, but she didn't dare ask. If she did, she'd worry it would get back to Zach and he might get the wrong idea.

"Mariah, can I see you for a second?"

She'd just walked into the clinic after a busy day of

farm calls, but Dr. Saffer's eyes smiled at her above his glasses in a way that reassured her. It had been over two months since she'd started. The doctor who'd been out on maternity was scheduled to return next month, and so she'd been expecting a conversation about her last day of work and so forth. It still depressed her. Well, depressed her even more than she'd been before. She kept her eyes on the white lab coat and followed him to his office behind the reception area.

"Sit down," he told her, motioning toward a chair in front of a beautiful wooden desk.

She loved this room. Tall ceilings, wide windows with a view of the low-lying mountains separating Via Del Caballo from the coast. Horse paintings: horse heads, rearing horses, running horses. Out in the wild. Galloping full tilt across a desert.

Where they might injure themselves.

Don't go there.

"Mariah, we have really enjoyed having you here."

Yup. This was it. The official "thank you for your service" speech. "I've enjoyed being here, too."

He had a pencil tucked behind his ear, the thing partially concealed by his gray hair. He pulled it out and set it on his desk almost as if her staring at it had made him recall its presence. He even smiled a bit.

"You are an amazing woman and a brilliant vet. That work you did with the racehorses, incredible. I understand from his owner that Summer is completely sound. Zach plans to race her this year."

Her stomach released a spasm that made her queasy. "That's great," she lied.

"We've received a number of referrals from the owner of that horse, a man I think you were seeing at one time?"

It was like swallowing lava rock. "I was."

"Not seeing him anymore?"

She shook her head.

"That's too bad. Seemed like a nice guy. I was thinking you might have been invited to watch his horse race this weekend."

She had been invited. In a way. "I'm going to catch it on TV."

Liar.

"Well, in any event, your work here has been exemplary. That's why I'd like to make it permanent."

She opened her mouth to tell him how much she'd enjoyed working there, how much she would miss it—but then his words penetrated. "Excuse me?"

Dr. Saffer smiled, clearly expecting her reaction. "Dr. Bowler has decided to stay home with her baby, at least until she gets a little older. That means we have an opening and we'd love for you to replace her."

Mariah was speechless, but then the breath left her because she'd been struck by an overwhelming urge to call Zach and tell him…only she couldn't.

"Oh, my goodness, Dr. Saffer, I don't know what to say." She was close to tears, although not for the reason her boss might think.

"Say yes."

"Yes!" she squeaked. "Of course, yes."

"Excellent." Dr. Saffer stood. "I can't tell you how pleased we are to have you on board, Mariah. I think your work with racehorses will bring this clinic to another level."

"Thank you."

You can't call him.

But she wanted to. Oh, how she wanted to.

"I'll announce it at our staff meeting tomorrow morning and then send out a press release this weekend." He held out his hand. "Congratulations."

"Thank you."

When she left the office, her hands shook. She should check in with the girls at the front desk. Instead she walked past them and to her car, where she climbed inside and bawled, just bawled, and not just because of the fantastic job offer. No, she cried because she missed Zach so terribly it felt like a physical pain. She wanted him to know how her life had just changed. She wanted to share her excitement. Wanted to jump up and down and whoop with excitement and celebrate…in Zach's arms.

Alas, he was no longer a part of her life.

When she got home that evening, she felt even more alone. The entire barn was at a horse show at the Santa Barbara showgrounds, an event where Dandy had made his debut, Zach's old horse picking up his first championship. It was in the baby greens, but there'd been a lot of talk about the fancy new hunter in the Uptown barn. She wouldn't be surprised if the new owner was offered big money for the gelding even with his old injury. The thought should have cheered her up. Happy ending all around. Only she wasn't happy. She was depressed to the point that she found herself walking aimlessly toward the barn. Nobody was around, not even Jillian. And those people who didn't have a horse showing weren't around, either. Tonight was the big Grand Prix. The crème de la crème of horses would be jumping in a big event, including Natalie's.

"To hell with it."

She would go and watch. Why not? It sure beat sitting around and moping.

So she got in her car and made the forty-five-minute

drive south. The Santa Barbara Grand Prix was scheduled for late evening, the sunset to her right reminding her of her evening with Zach.

Don't go there.

She didn't. She focused instead on the cars on the road. The closer she got to Santa Barbara, the more packed the roads became. The showgrounds were packed, too, but she'd been to the facility enough times to know the secret places to park. She timed it perfectly. Natalie should be out in the warm-up pen and she was certain Jillian would be out there with her. But the moment she walked between the wooden barns she could tell something was wrong. Natalie's horse, Nero, stood near the edge of the arena, with Jillian and Natalie's groom, Kate, standing nearby. Natalie was examining Nero's hoof. Mariah quickened her steps.

"What happened?"

Jillian turned and smiled. "Mariah!"

Her friend's response told her it was nothing serious. Mariah's shoulders relaxed. Natalie was picking something out of Nero's front foot. The horse's white sides were streaked with sweat even though it was cool outside. Behind them other riders warmed up, horses sailing over the warm-up fences, some of them being coached by people on the ground.

"Is he okay?"

"Fine," Natalie said, meeting her gaze. "Although he scared me half to death." She dropped Nero's foot and straightened. "There. That ought to feel better."

"She was out warming up when he suddenly pulled up lame." Jillian shook her head. "We all thought he'd hurt himself, but it turned out his foot was full of dirt."

"At least, I'm pretty sure that was it," Natalie said,

her pretty face dipping into a frown. "Kate, why don't you trot him out."

Uptown Farm's groom, a young girl as blonde as Natalie, nodded. She trotted the big warm blood off as Mariah eyed him critically.

"He looks fine now," she said, relieved.

"Thank goodness," Natalie said. "I thought at first he tore something."

"Me, too," Jillian echoed.

What Dandy does is just as risky as what Dasher does.

This was Nero, though, Mariah told herself. What he did was different than what Dandy would be doing.

He could still hurt himself.

"He's telling me he's okay," Jillian said.

She wished Jillian could tell her that she would be okay, Mariah thought.

Natalie climbed back on a moment later, looking the quintessential English rider in her dark blue hunt coat, breeches and black helmet. Mariah watched them closely when they trotted off, but it was clear the big horse was fine. In a moment they were back to jumping fences, but she could feel Jillian peeking glances at her.

Mariah tipped her chin up, but she didn't say anything right away. Natalie approached a fence and it was impossible not to hold her breath as the woman took the horse over a four-foot obstacle. She did it so perfectly.

"He looks good," she noted.

"Don't change the subject."

Another horse approached, but Mariah didn't watch nearly as closely. "As a matter of fact, I came here to celebrate."

Jillian eyed her skeptically. She placed her hands on

her jean-clad hips, the white T-shirt she wore pulling across her body.

"I was offered a full-time position at the clinic."

Jillian's whole face changed. "Mariah. That's great!"

She hugged her as Kate, who stood on the other side of her and hadn't heard, said, "What? What happened?"

"Mariah was offered a full-time position at the clinic," Jillian said, drawing back.

Kate's young face lit up, too. The girl was studying to be a vet. "Mariah, that's awesome."

It was awesome.

So why did she feel like crying?

"Mariah, what's wrong?"

She watched as Natalie took another fence, her horse like a gazelle, although he stumbled a bit on the other side. Natalie rode him like a pro.

"He's right, you know," Mariah said.

Kate went back to watching her boss, but Jillian held her gaze. "Who's right?"

She didn't want to admit it, she really didn't, but her momentary panic that Nero had been hurt had brought it all home. "A horse can get hurt at any time, anyplace."

To her surprise, Jillian didn't instantly disagree. "He promised you, though. He swore he wouldn't race Dasher if you helped him get well."

"Did he? I don't recall him ever promising not to race the horse. Unlike me. I promised him something once upon a time—and I broke that promise. He not only forgave me, he went on to help me later."

Out in the middle of the arena Natalie was patting Nero's neck. It was clear she was done warming up and that she was pleased with how Nero had performed.

"Look," Jillian said. "You know I'm not a big fan of

racing and that I was skeptical from the very beginning that you'd ever get through to Zach Johnson, much less his racing cronies."

"Don't remind me."

Jillian shook her head, "And I know you've been miserable since the two of you split up."

She couldn't look her friend in the eye. It was true.

"So I guess the big question is, are you more miserable with him—knowing what he does for a living—or when you're without him?"

Her mind went blank. Deep inside she knew the answer to that question.

Away from him.

"And the even bigger question," her friend continued, "do you love him enough to overlook what he does for a living?"

Love?

Was this love? This feeling that she couldn't breathe? The sick twist of her stomach when she'd seen Nero standing there, thinking he'd been hurt and realizing that Zach was right—a horse could get hurt anywhere, anytime.

"I'm pretty sure I know the answer to that question," Jillian said. "I think you know it, too."

Yes. She knew, but what would she do about it?

CHAOS.

It'd been a long time since the Triple J Stables had a horse in a stakes race, and he'd forgotten what it was like. Chaos. Long days at the track, media appearances and the obligatory parties and schmoozing with whatever muckety-muck happened to be throwing one. It wouldn't have been so bad but for the fact that the press had gotten wind of Dasher's miraculous recovery. That, combined with the fact that he'd won his last race in record time, made him the perfect Cinderella story during a slow news week.

"You going to the press conference, boss?"

Jose enjoyed the limelight and the horse he'd just hosed off was definitely a star. Dasher stood there tied outside his stall, eating from his hay net as if all the commotion were no big deal. Quarter horses. They had the best minds in the world. A Thoroughbred would have been pacing in his stall.

"Guess I have to go."

Jose smiled, revealing two gold teeth. The man had worked for Triple J for as long as Zach could remember. He'd been the first to notice something was wrong after Mariah had dumped him.

"Bit of a walk to the clubhouse," Jose said.

"Yup." And in the arid near-desert heat, he'd be miserable the whole way. "See you in a bit."

Miserable during the whole ordeal, too, but there was no way to get out of it. At least he wouldn't be alone. Wes had a horse entered, too, as did a couple of the other owners who called Golden Downs home. He wouldn't have to answer all the questions on his own. Maybe he'd get lucky and he wouldn't have to answer anything.

He should have known better.

The minute he walked in, all eyes turned in his direction. The pressroom overlooked the front stretch and it felt as if a hundred eyes followed his progress to the tables set up along the short side of the room. Network news, local news, equine journalists—they were all there.

"Wow," Zach said.

"Saved you a seat," Wes said, his green eyes full of amusement. "You do realize they're all here for you."

"No, they're not."

"Oh, yes, they are. Your horse was on the national news this morning. It's the feel-good story of the year, or at least this week. Down-on-his-luck racehorse owner gets a second chance at success with recovered race-horse."

"They're not here for me," he said again.

He was wrong. Again.

As soon as the president of the track opened up the floor for questions, all eyes turned to him.

"Zach, Zach. Here, here." Hands waved; cameras clicked; recorders were switched on. Zach blinked spots out of his eyes and selected the familiar female face. Well, he thought it might be familiar. He was so blinded by flashes he could barely see.

"Zach," Christine Hamilton asked, "how does it feel to have a horse entered in your first major stakes race in years?"

Yup. He'd picked the right woman. Blond hair and a friendly smile. "Twelve years, to be exact, but who's counting? And it feels great."

"Zach, Zach," a man called. Zach didn't recognize him. "How did you feel when you realized your horse might have a shot at winning the Million Dollar Futu-rity?"

He shook his head in disbelief. "Thrilled. Nervous. Still nervous," he said with a laugh.

"Are you worried your horse will break down?" some-one else called, a man he recognized from television.

"I was at first, but Black in a Dash hasn't taken an off step since I brought him home. And actually, this is a good time to thank Dr. Mariah Stewart and the staff at Via Del Caballo Veterinary Clinic for taking such excellent care of my stallion. Dr. Stewart was amazing. We wouldn't be here today without her."

"Will she be watching the race with you tonight?" someone else asked.

"Alas, no. Dr. Stewart isn't a big fan of the sport." He hoped he hid his disappointment. "She does what she does out of love of horses, nothing more."

"Actually, that's not precisely true."

He thought he heard wrong. That had sounded like...

He scanned the crowd, hoping, wondering, calling himself a fool because there was no way—

Mariah.

She smiled at him from the back row and Zach's heart just about flipped over in his chest.

"I actually *will* be watching." Her smile reminded him of the time Erin had called him Mariah's boyfriend, her smile somewhat abashed but also determined. "I just don't know if I'll be in the owners' box."

He didn't know what to say. He knew what he wanted to *do.* He wanted to jump over the table and pull her into her arms, but he'd have to knock down a few people in order to do that. He cleared his throat.

"Ladies and gentlemen," he heard himself say, "my veterinarian, Dr. Mariah Stewart, the woman who saved Dasher's leg."

Cameras turned in Mariah's direction. Flashes white-washed her face. Someone thrust a mic in front of her.

"Dr. Stewart, is this your first time watching a race?"

"Dr. Stewart, can you tell us a little about Dasher's therapy?"

"Dr. Stewart, is it true you dumped my friend?"

The last came from Wes and Zach wanted to kill him. Wes had managed to do what celebrities could only dream of doing—silence a roomful of reporters.

"Wes," he hissed.

Mariah lifted a hand in Zach's direction. "Why, yes, Wes. That's true."

"Because you disagreed with him about putting Dasher in this race."

"Yes."

Zach covered his mic and leaned toward Wes. "What are you doing?"

Wes covered his mic, too. "Getting the two of you to talk. Lord knows you're both so stubborn you'll probably say something stupid."

The people in the room must have sensed a story unfolding, because they held their tongues.

With a complacent smile, Wes uncovered his mic. "So what are you doing here now, Dr. Stewart?"

"Well, I—" She glanced around the room and Zach could see her cheeks color. She didn't want to answer, he could tell, would have preferred to talk to him privately. But then she lifted her chin. "I *still* think it's a mistake, but as someone once said, Black in a Dash could reinjure himself out in a pasture. So I'm here now because if he does reinjure himself, I'm his vet and I want to be here for him."

"So you're going to watch the race now?" a reporter asked.

Zach held his breath.

"Only if I can stand next to Dasher's owner."

Zach shot to his feet. Mariah smiled. He started to move around the table. It was like the parting of the Red Sea. Journalists moved out of the way. Camera crews.

Race fans. Mariah stepped forward. Zach would never remember moving in her direction. All he knew was that one minute she was in the back and the next she was in his arms.

"What are you doing here?" he asked softly.

There were tears in her eyes. "They hired me full-time at the clinic and all I could think about afterward was how much I wanted to see you, only I couldn't, because I was so wrapped up in who I was supposed to be—Mariah the activist—that I couldn't see the forest through the trees, but then I thought you were right, I was being a hypocrite, because just the other day one of Natalie's horses hurt itself coming off a fence and I found myself thinking—"

"For God's sake, just kiss her," Wes's voice blared over the microphone.

Zach glanced in his friend's direction, winked and did exactly that. He didn't care that there was a roomful of journalists watching. Didn't mind that his peers from Golden Downs looked on. Wasn't bothered by the sudden flash of a bulb, then another and another. All he could think about was that Mariah was here, at the track, in his arms and he was kissing her and she kissed him back.

"I love you," she murmured against his lips. "I tried so hard to fight it, but I just couldn't do it."

"Shh," he soothed.

"Whatever happens to Dasher tonight, I promise to be there for you, Zach."

"The only thing you're going to have to do is stand next to me in the winner's circle."

"I hope so. I really do hope your dream comes true."

He touched the side of her face, a gesture he'd done a

million times and that he knew he'd do a million more times. "Mariah, my dream already *has* come true."

She smiled. He kissed her again, and later that night, when Dasher crossed the finish line first, setting a new track record, Zach kissed her again, just as he kissed her on their wedding day, the day when *both* their dreams came true.

* * * * *

Be sure to look for Pamela Britton's next book set in the horse community of Via Del Caballo, California, available in 2015 from Harlequin American Romance!

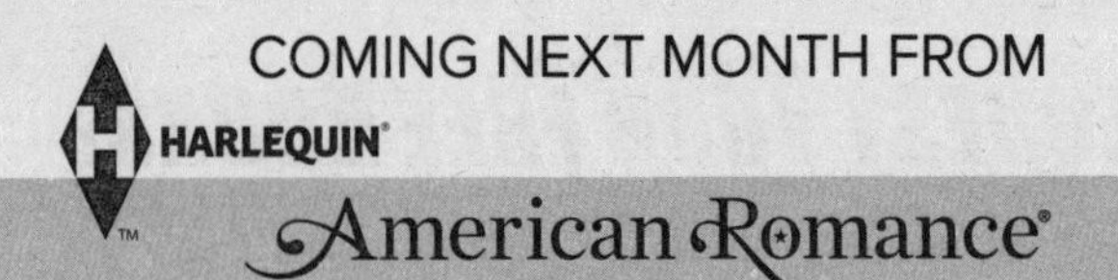

Available May 6, 2014

#1497 ONE NIGHT IN TEXAS

by Linda Warren

Telling the truth about her child's paternity could destroy Angie Wiznowski's relationship with her daughter *and* her daughter's father. But it was a secret Hardison Hollister was never meant to know....

#1498 THE COWBOY'S DESTINY

The Cash Brothers

by Marin Thomas

Destiny Saunders is pregnant and determined to raise her baby on her own. When cowboy Buck Cash arrives in town, Destiny knows nothing can happen between them. Even if she really wants it to!

#1499 A BABY FOR THE DOCTOR

Safe Harbor Medical

by Jacqueline Diamond

Handsome surgeon Jack Ryder had a reputation as a ladies' man until he met the one woman who refused to be impressed: nurse Anya Meeks. She's carrying his baby—and she's determined to give it up for adoption.

#1500 THE BULL RIDER'S FAMILY

Glade County Cowboys

by Leigh Duncan

Chef Emma Shane took a job on the Circle P Ranch to provide a quiet home for her young daughter. But former bull rider Colt Judd is making her life there anything but peaceful!

Looking for more exciting all-American romances like the one you just read? Read on for an excerpt from THE COWBOY'S DESTINY by Marin Thomas

Destiny Saunders marched down the aisle and poked her head out the door.

Blast you, Daryl.

Even though they'd known each other only six months, she hadn't expected him to leave her high and dry. She rubbed her belly. At barely two months pregnant it would be several weeks before she showed.

She left the chapel, closing the doors behind her. After stowing her purse and phone, she slid on her mirrored sunglasses and straddled the seat of her motorcycle, revving the engine to life. Then she tore out of the parking lot, tires spewing gravel.

She'd driven only two miles when she spotted a pickup parked on the shoulder of the road.

A movement caught her attention, and she zeroed in on the driver's-side window, out of which stuck a pair of cowboy boots. She approached the vehicle cautiously and peered through the open window, finding a cowboy sprawled inside, his hat covering his face.

She slapped her hand against the bottom of one boot then jumped when the man bolted into an upright position, knocking his forehead against the rearview mirror.

"Need a lift?"

He glanced at her outfit. "Where's the groom?"

"If I knew that, I wouldn't be talking to you right now."

He shoved his hand out the window. "Buck Cash."

"Destiny Saunders. Where are you headed?"

"Up to Flagstaff for a rodeo this weekend," he replied as he got out of the vehicle.

"What's wrong with your truck?"

"Puncture in one of the hoses."

He peered over her shoulder and she caught a whiff of his cologne. A quiver that had nothing to do with morning sickness spread through her stomach.

"Guess you're going to miss your rodeo," she said.

"There's always another one." He eyed the bike. "This your motorcycle?"

"You think I ditched my fiancé at the altar and then took off on his bike?"

"Kind of looks that way." He kept a straight face but his eyes sparkled.

"Looks can be deceiving. Hop on."

Look for THE COWBOY'S DESTINY
by Marin Thomas in
May 2014 wherever books and ebooks are sold

HAREXP0514